WITHDRAWN

MUTANT BUNNY ISLAND #3

BUNS OF STEEL

BY OBERT SKYE

ILLUSTRATED BY EDUARDO VIEIRA

HARPER

An Imprint of HarperCollinsPublishers

Mutant Bunny Island #3: Buns of Steel
Copyright © 2019 by HarperCollins Publishers
All rights reserved. Printed in the United States of America.
No part of this book may be used or reproduced in any manner whatsoever without written
permission except in the case of brief quotations embodied in critical articles and reviews. For
information address HarperCollins Children's Books, a division of HarperCollins Publishers,
195 Broadway, New York, NY 10007.
www.harpercollinschildrens.com

Library of Congress Cataloging-in-Publication Data

Names: Skye, Obert, author. | Vieira, Eduardo (Illustrator), illustrator.
Title: Buns of steel / by Obert Skye ; illustrated by Eduardo Vieira.
Description: First edition. | New York, NY : Harper, an imprint of HarperCollins Publishers,
    [2019] | Series: Mutant Bunny Island ; #3 | Summary: Shortly after he lands on Bunny Island
    for vacation, eleven-year-old Perry Owen discovers hostile robot rabbits, but will his friends and
    family believe him in time to save the island from destruction?
Identifiers: LCCN 2019000129 | ISBN 9780062399175 (hardcover)
Subjects: | CYAC: Rabbits--Fiction. | Islands--Fiction. | Mystery and detective stories. |
    Humorous stories.
Classification: LCC PZ7.S62877 Bu 2019 | DDC [Fic]--dc23 LC record available at
    https://lccn.loc.gov/2019000129
ISBN 978-0-06-239917-5

Typography by Joe Merkel
19 20 21 22 23 PC/LSCH 10 9 8 7 6 5 4 3 2 1
❖

First Edition

To my brother, Jeff
There are few people in the world I like more.
Thanks for being so OG and so Jeffish.
—Obert Skye

To my mother, who showed me
that real heroes do exist! Miss you, Mom.
—Eduardo Vieira

CHAPTER ONE

PAWS AND PAS

The plane bounced as it flew through the air. Out my window I couldn't see anything besides blue sky. I have no problem with blue sky, but I'd rather I was a squid traveling through the ocean. Luckily, I was heading back to a spot on the globe where there would be plenty of ocean. Unluckily, the plane ride was bumpy. Not that the bumps were making me nervous—something else was. You see, leaving Ohio used to give me jittery legs, but this was my third trip to my uncle Zeke's home and I felt like a pro. What made me nervous was that for the first time I was making the journey with my dad. He was in the seat next to me, reading a book called *The Cauliflower Caper.*

I love my dad, but there are times when he can be embarrassing. For example, like the time he was sitting next to me reading a book about cauliflower.

My dad looked up from his book and smiled at me. His big mustache wriggled, and the lines on his forehead scrunched up and then disappeared.

Since I was eleven, I was also a little too cool to smile back. So I nodded and pushed my brown hair up off my forehead. My fingers got caught in my hair, and I ended up yanking a bunch of strands out. Okay, maybe I'm not that cool.

My dad went back to reading.

Here are the deets. My dad and I live alone. My mother died when I was three, and since then it has been just us. I have no brothers or sisters, and no pets. My father and I don't always see eye to eye, but he tries hard to be the kind of dad a squid cadet like me needs. Two days ago, he surprised me by announcing that we were going to Bunny Island together. It was Bunny Break on the island, and my dad had earned enough miles on his credit card to pay for the tickets. I was flipper-gasted! We'd never gone on a big trip together before, and my dad had never been to Bunny Island.

It seemed like a good idea.

But now, as I sat next to him, I was growing worried. I had friends on Bunny Island. It was sort of my place.

There was a very good chance that my dad would cramp my style. I thought I wanted to share the island with him, but I also knew how painful sharing can be.

My dad closed his book and then blew his nose loudly into his handkerchief.

"Planes make me phlegmy," he said with a smile.

Yes, I was definitely worried about the wisdom of bringing him along.

"So, Uncle Zeke really doesn't know we're coming?" I asked as my dad tucked his handkerchief back into the pocket on the front of his shirt.

"No," he replied. "I want to surprise him. He was always surprising me when we were kids. One time he filled my shoes with Jell-O."

"And this trip is to get him back?"

"Also, to spend some quality outdoor time with my son."

The worry grew.

"I'm sure my friends will want to hang out with me most of the time," I warned him.

"Great. We can all hang out together," he warned me.

By the time we landed, I had almost convinced myself that things were going to be fine. But then as we were walking through the airport, my dad kept waving at everyone and embarrassing me.

"Do you know that person?" I asked.

"Not yet."

Nobody waved back. I don't blame them—my dad looked like a seal who couldn't control his flippers. Plus, the outfit he was wearing was outdated. He had on a large wide-brimmed hat, a floral shirt, white shorts that needed to be a couple of inches longer, white tennis shoes he had bought thirty years ago, blue socks that came up to just under his knees, and a fluffy bunny tail that he had been given when we got off the plane stuck to the back of his pants. Somehow he managed to look more ridiculous than all the other out-of-touch Bunny Mooners who visited the island.

As we exited the airport, my dad saw some posters on the doors and stopped to read them. The posters welcomed visitors to the island and invited everyone to have a fun but safe Bunny Break.

"Fun but safe," my dad said. "I like that."

There was a smaller poster with information about a bun-fire they would be having on the beach in a couple of days.

"Maybe we should go to that?" my dad suggested.

"I do like fire."

Stepping out of the airport, we got our first great view of the island. Everything looked beautiful—the flowers were in bloom, the birds were singing, and the ocean sat like a blue jewel in the far distance. Things looked like I remembered, all except the sky. It was an unusual shade of purple that I had never seen before.

My dad breathed in the warm tropical air.

"I'm going to need to moisturize my nostrils," he said. "This warm wind will dry them out for sure."

Usually I don't go out in public with my dad. Typically, I find any excuse I can to stay home. I like to stay indoors and close to my comics and computer. I never go grocery shopping with my dad or to the mall or to the movies. We don't go camping or on many vacations or spend time at museums. We both enjoy just hanging around our house and doing what we like. Occasionally, we'll watch TV together or play board games. Sometimes he forces me to go out into the backyard, where he throws various balls at me until one of them accidentally hits my face and causes my nose to bleed.

I honestly can't remember the last time I've done something outside our house with him. Now, as he talked about his dry nostrils in public, I was reminded why.

The scene outside was not only beautiful—it was busy. Tourists were running around the front of the airport. There were some people driving golf carts up and down Rabbit Road, and a few were rolling around on Segways. On the ground there were hundreds and hundreds of bunnies. Some were hopping, some were sitting, and some were shuffling across the landscape like fuzzy splotches with floppy ears. My dad gently nudged a brown one near him with the toe of his shoe. The bunny looked up but didn't move.

"You're a nice-looking kitten," he cooed.

"This isn't Cat Island," I informed him.

"Baby bunnies are called kittens."

"Right," I said, having forgotten that. "Well, there are way more rabbits here than I remember."

The two of us gazed out toward the ocean. I could see the long Rabbit Road as it ran directly toward the sea. I saw the Bunny Hotel with the large bunny statue on top of it and the hundreds and hundreds of palm trees that lined the road, their long leaves swaying slowly in the warm, weak wind. There were Bunny Mooners carefully driving golf carts around as they tried to avoid the bunnies.

"Seriously," I whispered. "I can barely see the ground."

"Rabbits can multiply quickly," my father said. "Now, is that our hotel way down there?"

My dad pointed down Rabbit Road to the Bunny Hotel with the big bunny statue on top. The statue had recently been painted gold, and it stood out against the purple sky.

"That's it," I said, feeling sheepish.

Every local knows that the Bunny Hotel is for tourists and Bunny Mooners. It's not the kind of place someone who has saved the island twice stays. Not that it isn't nice; it's just not cool.

The two of us slowly dragged our suitcases behind us as we walked down the stone path toward the hotel while constantly pushing bunnies out of the way.

Two old and rich-looking Bunny Mooners almost knocked us over as they rushed to take pictures of a large black rabbit near us.

Bunny Island had grown in popularity since the first time I had come, and not to brag, but my friends and I sort of had a lot to do with that. The stories and rumors about mutant bunnies and giant rabbits have made the place larger-than-life. It also made it more crowded. Port O'Hare on the other side of the island was bringing in cruises filled with people who just wanted to see the places mentioned in the stories and to witness all the thousands of bunnies on the ground.

"We should hurry and check into our hotel," my dad insisted while shooing a bunny off the path. "I don't want them to worry."

"I don't think the hotel will worry," I told him. "But I did tell my friends to meet me there at four."

We walked over and around hundreds of hares. For some reason, the rabbits weren't getting out of the way like they usually did. They just sat there, twitching their whiskers and ears and making us maneuver carefully. A big fat yellow one was sitting in front of me, and it didn't flinch as I got closer. I leaned down to pick it up and lift it out of the way, but it growled and its eyes flashed angrily.

"Whoa." I backed away quickly.

"Aren't bunnies supposed to be adorable?" my dad asked with concern.

"I don't know what's up with him," I said as I stepped over the demented rabbit.

When we got to the Bunny Hotel there was a man in a bellhop uniform standing under the overhang by the front door. He was pushing away bunnies so that people could walk in without the animals coming in.

The woman at the front desk had incredibly thick glasses on and a pile of curly blond hair stacked up on top of her head. There were green, grassy-looking earrings dangling from her earlobes, and her lips were painted a shade of red that flattered her brown eyes and dark skin. If I had to guess, I would say she was old, like my dad. She looked up from what she was doing to welcome us.

"Hello, my name is Summer. Welcome to the Bunny Hotel."

"We feel welcomed," my dad said. "I hope we didn't keep you waiting. The name's Zane Owens."

Summer began to type on her keyboard while staring at me as if I had boogers in my nose or food on my face.

"Sorry," she said. "Aren't you that boy?"

I was afraid of this. I had become quite famous on Bunny Island. So her noticing me made perfect sense. After all, my friends and I had saved the place a couple of times. Because of that I was like a local celebrity, and now I had been recognized again.

"Guilty," I said, trying to act humble.

"You know him?" my dad asked her with surprise. "Perry, you never told me you were acquainted with such a charming person."

"No, Dad," I said embarrassed. "She recognizes me from saving the island before."

"What?" Summer sounded confused. "You saved the island? I thought you were the kid in my neighborhood who ate that cardboard box on a dare last week."

Both my dad and Summer looked at me.

"Cardboard actually has some nutritional value," my dad said, turning to face her. "It can be a good source of fiber."

Okay, I could be wrong—no, no, I wish I was wrong—but Summer was smiling at my dad and acting like what he was saying made sense.

"I have a nephew who eats dirt," she replied. "He says it has minerals."

Now it was my dad's turn to smile at her.

"Your nephew's right. Dirt is underrated. At least

once a year, I take a dirt bath. It does wonders for the skin. I soil myself to stay youthful looking."

My dad's choice of words was unfortunate, but Summer kept looking at him as if a conversation about people soiling themselves was acceptable.

"Go on," she said.

My head felt dizzy. I don't know what was happening, but for some gross reason my dad and Summer were locking eyes and smiling like the two dopey spectacle-porpoises in *Ocean Blasterzoids* Issue #21: "The Porpoise of Love."

"Um, Dad," I spoke up. "We should check in."

"Right," he said to Summer. "And I need to find moisturizer for my nostrils. This sea air is making them scaly."

It would have been fine if the weird-colored skies had opened up and I had been struck with lightning. At least then I wouldn't have to endure my father's nostril talk.

"We sell moisturizer in the hotel store," Summer said lovingly.

"What a wonderful place," my dad replied.

"There's also going to be a mixer in the Angora Room in a few minutes," she announced. "Just people mingling and socializing. There will be carrot-aid and carrot cake served."

"I do like vegetable-based cakes," my dad admitted.

Summer smiled so wide, I thought the edges of her mouth were going to pop off the sides of her face. She then handed my dad our room keys.

"I gave you a room with one of the best views," she said. "You can see both the ocean and the Volcanto mountain range."

"I look forward to staring at both things." My father paused to point at his own eyes. "I want to *see* everything while I'm here."

"You should," she said excitedly. "If you like, there are a number of pamphlets by the elevator that show some of the attractions and natural wonders on the island. I think there's one about Volcanto."

My dad thanked her for all her help, and as we walked away she hollered.

"I *hop* your stay is enjoyable!"

My dad stopped and smiled at her. "It's already been very *bun*."

I wanted to crawl into one of the thousands of bunny holes on the island and never come out. My dad was more embarrassing than a young squid accidentally inking himself in front of a school of fish.

Instead of crawling into a hole, however, I waited as my father gathered dozens of tourist pamphlets from the rack. We then got into the elevator and headed up to our room.

CHAPTER TWO
DECEPTION AND SECRETS

I brushed my teeth and tried to comb my hair a little before going to the lobby to meet Juliet. My brown hair was short and a little puffy, but the red *Ocean Blasterzoids* T-shirt I was wearing brought out the blue in my eyes.

Juliet had not replied to the emails I had sent yesterday telling her that I was coming, so there was a solid chance she wouldn't show. But at four o'clock exactly, and while I was standing by a big green vase in the lobby, someone slipped up behind me and put their hands over my eyes.

"Guess who?"

I knew it was Juliet, but I decided to flatter her by pretending her hands were as soft as the nubbins on a seahorse.

"Stacy Horse?"

Juliet laughed. "Of course you would say something ridiculous like that."

I turned around and there she was. I wasn't sure what to do. We had become good friends thanks to the adventures we had gone through and the problems we had solved. We had even held hands a couple of times. Also, I had told everyone back in Ohio that she was my girlfriend—whether she knew that or not, I couldn't tell. Now, as I saw her, I wondered if we should hug or bow or click.

I have no idea how to act around girls.

Leaning forward, I reached out and tapped Juliet on her right shoulder with my left hand.

As usual, Juliet didn't care about what I did. She gave me a real hug with no clicking or bowing or loss of dignity.

Juliet looked as cool as any squid or seahorse I had ever seen or read about. Her popcorn-colored hair was a little shorter than when I had last seen her—coming down to just below her chin. The green in her eyes looked dark and deep, like the color of kelp. Her lips were covered with some sort of sparkly lip gloss that made her shine even brighter than she usually did. She was wearing a red tank top, white shorts, and sandals that showed off her purple-painted toenails. I probably should have spent more time combing my hair or choosing what I was wearing. Because the Admiral Uli T-shirt and my cargo shorts I had on suddenly seemed a little less impressive now that I could see how she looked.

"When I checked my email at the library this morning, I was thrilled," she said. "I can't believe you're here. And you brought your dad?"

"Yes. He's in the room washing up and combing his mustache. I think he's hoping to impress the woman working at the front desk."

"Summer?"

I nodded while trying to stand as tall as I could. I don't know what it was, but Juliet was making me wish I had done a few push-ups today. She also had my head feeling as light as the Puffer, Admiral Uli's enemy in *Ocean Blasterzoids* Issue #66: "The Deadly Buoy."

"Are you okay?" Juliet asked. "You look a little pale."

"That's because squids have the ability to blend into their scenery," I said as I stood in front of a white wall. "I have something for you."

Needing a distraction, I pulled out a small blue box from one of the big pockets in my cargo shorts. Juliet would no longer notice how pale I was when she saw the present I brought her.

"What's that?" she asked as I handed her the box.

"Just something I found at my house," I replied.

Juliet opened the box and pulled out a gold necklace that used to belong to my mom. It had a thin gold chain with a small gold moon hanging from it. I had found it in a drawer at my house, and my dad had given me permission to give it to her.

"It's amazing," Juliet whispered.

She handed me the box and put the necklace on. I'm pretty sure she was going to hug me again or go on about what a great person I was, but we were interrupted by someone punching me on the right shoulder.

"Oww."

I turned to see Rain. Punching me was something he did occasionally. He thought it was friendly; I thought it was a sign of mental instability.

"Hi, Perry," he said. He then made a gesture of kindness by extending his right hand so that we could execute our custom handshake.

"Tentacles, tentacles, shark fin, shark fin, blowhole." We both said the words while bumping our fists, slapping our hands, and then exploding our fingers.

Rain was the kind of person who looked cool just standing there. He had brown skin and broad shoulders. His bangs were wavy and long and hung down over his right eye—leaving his left eye to look at the things he deemed worthy of looking at. He was wearing a white tank top that said Rain Train on it. Rain was also two

years older than me and Juliet and ran a business trans-
porting people around on his bike.

"Did you bring me something?" Rain asked as he
looked at Juliet wearing the necklace.

I handed him the empty box. "Here."

"Is it some sort of invisible squid thing?" Rain asked
as he looked at the small box.

"Yes," I replied. "And you're welcome."

Rain and I had a complicated relationship. We were
friends, but we were the kind of friends that no one
would ever design. On paper it didn't look like we would
get along, but thanks to the things we had been through
and me saving his butt a few times, we got along.

"So, have either of you seen Zeke lately?"

Both my friends suddenly looked guilty.

"What?" I asked.

"Nothing," Juliet said. "Of course we've seen him."

"He's still dating my mom," Rain added. "But he's
really . . . busy."

The way Juliet and Rain were speaking made it sound
like they wanted to say more than they were.

I stared at them. "Is something wrong?"

"No," Juliet said unconvincingly. "Nothing's wrong. I
mean, it's Bunny Break and you're here. Things seem just
like they should."

I looked at Juliet and then at Rain.

"Okay then," I said. "Well, Zeke doesn't know we're here. My dad wanted to surprise him."

"Oh, he'll be surprised," Rain insisted.

"I'm going to his house to see if he's there."

Rain and Juliet looked at each other again.

"What?" I asked with frustration.

"Nothing," Juliet insisted while fiddling with the necklace around her neck.

"Then you'll come with me?" I asked.

"Now?" Juliet said. "I wanted to meet your dad."

"You don't want to see him yet. He's washing up," I told her. "We'll go get Zeke and bring him back here. That way my dad can surprise him."

"I should get back to my business," Rain said. "But since all my bikes are rented out at the moment, I guess I can break away."

"All your bikes?" I asked, confused.

"Rain has six bikes now," Juliet said. "He even has a little stand back behind the mall where he rents them out."

"Well, I wish we had some to ride to Zeke's," I complained.

"You know, he might not be home," Juliet said.

"If he's not, he probably left a note. Admiral Uli always leaves a note, and Zeke is one of the most squid-like people I know."

Rain smiled. "I'm glad you're back, Perry."

"Save your praise for later," I insisted.

I ran up to my room to tell my dad where I was going. He was busy applying lotion to his elbows and nose. I was glad I had not brought my friends up with me.

"Have fun out there," he said. "Bring your uncle back and I'll be ready to surprise him. Do you think I should jump out from behind something like a plant?"

"Go with what your fish guts tell you," I answered. "That's what Uli always does."

"Good advice."

I left my dad and ran back to the lobby. My friends and I then exited the Bunny Hotel and headed out into the rabbit-infested world.

CHAPTER THREE
WRONG PEOPLE IN THE RIGHT PLACE

We walked down Rabbit Road toward the ocean. Everywhere I looked there were Bunny Mooners and tourists milling about and walking in and out of shops and restaurants. The island seemed at least three times more populated than before. There were so many rabbits, we had to zigzag.

"The island's so crowded," I complained.

"It's Bunny Break," Juliet said happily.

A couple of locals sitting on a bench by the mall saw me and my friends and waved.

"Is the island in trouble again?" one of them yelled out to us.

"No trouble," Rain yelled back. "Perry's just here for a visit."

The bunnies around our feet and on the road were getting thicker. I looked back over my shoulder and saw big patches of them hopping behind us.

"What's going on with the rabbits?" I complained. "There're so many."

"You've just forgotten what it's like," Juliet said. "There're always this many."

"That's not true. We never had to work our way around like this. And look, I think some are following us."

"You're being paranoid," Rain insisted. "There're no more purple carrots that turn people into mutant bunnies or giant bunnies that want to capture us. There're just a lot of rabbits because it's Bunny Island."

"Really? Because I think there're a bunch following us." I looked back at the large patch of rabbits behind us.

"Paranoid," Rain repeated.

When we got to the beach at the end of Rabbit Road, I saw a large wooden bunny that they were preparing for the bun-fire. It was fifteen feet tall and shaped like a fat rabbit. There were people nailing on boards to make the ears on top.

"It's pretty good," I said. "And they're just going to burn it down?"

"They do it every year at the end of the break," Juliet informed me.

We turned left and walked along the shore until we eventually passed the glass phone booth near the Gray Hare subdivision where my uncle lived. It was the same phone booth I had first met Juliet at.

My uncle's neighborhood looked just like it had always looked. There were a bunch of mismatched little homes dotting the landscape. Some looked new and modern, while others looked like they were old and had been built in a hurry and without much of a budget.

Zeke's home was small, square, and yellow, like a giant Lego brick. It had a multicolored roof that looked purple and orange under the clear sky. His mailbox was shaped like a fat pelican, and the front door of the house was a faded color of green. There was also a carving of a squid on the door.

After knocking, we quickly discovered that Zeke was not there. To make things worse, somebody else was there—a young couple who both had yellow hair, and wore tight jeans, and baggy T-shirts. They answered the door like they owned the place and informed us that they were renting the house for the week.

"It was listed on Carrot's List," the blond boy said.

"Carrot's List?" I said, disgusted.

"That's a website for people to rent out their homes or sell stuff on Bunny Island," Juliet explained as the two blond renters stared at us. "Tons of people are renting out their homes to Bunny Mooners and tourists these days. The island's so popular."

"So, this is your uncle's house?" the blond girl asked me.

I nodded.

"Could you tell him that the bathroom's really small?" she complained.

"Yeah," the man said. "And the towels could be fluffier. That's why we'll be giving the place only a two-carrot review online."

"Sorry about the towels," I said insincerely. "I don't suppose you know where my uncle is?"

"I don't even know who he is," she said. "We rented this through the app, the same app we'll leave the bad review on."

Not only was I bothered that my uncle wasn't where he was supposed to be, but I was also bothered that I had to talk to these people. Juliet, Rain, and I left my uncle's house and walked down the street back toward the entrance of the Gray Hare subdivision.

"I don't understand," I said. "Zeke would never let people like that stay in his house."

"Maybe he wants to make some extra money," Rain

said. "Seriously, everyone's doing it."

As usual, Rain seemed to be living in a fantasy world that didn't include things like evil newts that infiltrated people's homes using annoying blond-haired people.

"If Zeke's renting his house, then where's he living?"

Out of the corner of my eye I could see Rain and Juliet look at each other and shake their heads.

"I saw that." I stopped walking to glare at them. "You two know something. You . . . Wait a second," I said, slapping my forehead. "Are your tentacles tingling?"

"No," my friends said.

"Well, mine are, and I think Zeke's probably with your mom, Flower. We should go to the Liquid Love Shack."

I started walking down the shore again, but this time my steps were bigger, and I was moving with purpose. Juliet and Rain followed closely behind.

"I don't think he's with my mom," Rain tried.

"Really?" I said. "Why wouldn't . . ."

As I looked back to talk to Rain, I noticed that once again there was a large herd of bunnies hopping behind us.

I stopped walking and the rabbits stopped too.

"Look at that," I said as I pointed. "That's not normal."

We started to walk again, and the bunnies slowly hopped in sync behind us like a mobile mound of fuzz.

"Okay," Juliet admitted. "That's a lot of rabbits."

The three of us began to walk faster and the bunnies

increased their speed.

We exited the Gray Hare subdivision and passed the phone booth. I thought about climbing on top of it, but I didn't know if I had the skills to do that. To the left of us was open beach. It was empty and there were no other humans in the area.

The bunny mound behind us began to make a clicking noise.

We stepped up over a small rock curb and onto the sandy beach. I was hoping that the bunnies would just give up and go their own way, but they continued to follow us. All their whiskers were twitching, and their tails shook as they hopped.

"I wish there was someone around we could scream to," I said.

"Up there!" Rain yelled.

Rain pointed toward an empty lifeguard tower near the edge of the water. It was a small raised platform made of wood and covered in faded blue paint. There was no lifeguard on duty and it had a sign that said *Stay Off.*

All three of us ignored the sign and climbed up the wooden steps and onto the platform. Looking down, we saw hundreds of bunnies closing in around the base of the lifeguard station. Some began to hop up the stairs, so Rain started to kick and swat at them with his feet.

"What is happening?" Juliet yelled. "They seem possessed."

Bunnies began to claw at the sand around the station.

"I can't stop them forever!" Rain hollered as he kicked.

"They're tearing the ground up," I hollered back.

"Look!" Juliet said loudly. "They're chewing at the base of the wood."

She was right: the rabbits were clawing and biting the wooden beams that were holding the raised platform up. Sand and splinters were flying everywhere. I looked down and could see that the waves were only a few feet away from where we were. If we jumped over the ring of rabbits, we might be able to escape into the water.

I screamed my idea to my friends.

"What other option do we have?" Juliet screamed back. "This thing won't stay up much longer."

Whump!

There was the sound of something collapsing, followed by the chatter and clicking of a thousand bunnies. We thought the platform would soon fall over, but then the waves flooded in and the ground became soft and just gave way. With one giant swoosh, all the attack bunnies were sucked down into the beach right in front of us.

"Now!" Rain ordered.

We jumped down off the back of the lifeguard chair, over the few bunnies still left, and then leaped over the edge of the hole that had already started to fill with muddy water.

"Run!"

Rain's suggestion was good but unnecessary. Juliet and I were already tearing down the beach, racing toward where the bun-fire was being set up.

"Maybe I shouldn't have come back to the island," I yelled.

"That's what I was thinking!" Rain yelled back.

I saw a short man and a wide woman coming down the stone path near Rabbit Road. They had on their swimsuits and were heading toward the ocean.

"Stay back!" I warned them. "Bunnies!"

I looked around and realized that there were no rabbits chasing us and the ones nearby were acting like they should.

"Bunnies?" the short man said as if I were joking. "There're bunnies everywhere."

"I think you've gotten too much sun," a woman wearing bunny ears and a bunny-print summer dress added. "Bunnies are nothing to scream about."

"Eeeeeek!" another woman screeched as she bent down to pick up a small orange bunny that was sitting on the ground near her. "Such a wuvy, wuvy, wuv," she cooed into the poor bunny's face.

"Come on!" Juliet said, taking my hand. "We need to find Zeke."

"That's what I've been saying."

The three of us ran up the stone path until we found a private spot beneath a tall palm tree.

"What was that?" I asked while trying to catch my breath.

"Frightening," Juliet answered.

"See, this is why we need Zeke," I argued.

"Okay," Juliet gave in. "We know where your uncle is."

"You do?"

"It's not good," Juliet said.

"Is he okay?" I panicked.

"Sort of," Juliet assured me. "But he made us promise we wouldn't tell you."

"Tell him I gave you a squid pinch and forced you to tell me the truth."

"Squid pinch?" Rain said.

"It's where you take your tentacles and apply pressure to the right side of the neck or gills to make your enemies tell you the truth. It was first used in Issue . . ." I stopped talking because both my friends were looking at me like I had newties.

"Fine," I complained. "Just take me to Zeke?"

I followed my friends farther into the palm trees.

CHAPTER FOUR

FIRST-MATE DISAPPOINTMENT

"I don't understand," I said loudly. "You two know where Zeke is—why didn't you just tell me?"

My friends and I were running on a sandy path that wound through palm trees, past the police station, and near the library.

"We were sworn to secrecy," Rain explained.

"Like Uli?" I said with excitement. "Like when he found out the cod code to the trout treasure?"

"Yes," Juliet added. "Exactly like that."

"Stop talking about trout treasure," Rain said. "What was up with those bunnies? Why were they attacking us?"

"We're lucky the tide came in when it did," Juliet said, still fiddling with her necklace. "And that huge sinkhole formed out of nowhere."

"It's because of all the burrows," Rain said. "The rabbits have been digging up everything under the island, making the ground unstable."

"It seems like the whole island is a little whack," I added. "The sky's the wrong color, my dad was flirting with the hotel woman, and now the bunnies have gone mad."

Juliet turned onto a new path that was practically blocked with bunnies. There were also Bunny Mooners driving golf carts carefully down it. We ran between two carts and up to a large black building. I recognized the building, but I had never been in it. It was easy to remember because it was the tallest building on the whole island. It was seven stories tall and belonged to the Crosshair Corporation. I knew that part only because of the big silver letters on the outside.

"Why are we going here?"

"You'll see."

We shooed bunnies away from the front door and entered the building. Inside there was a large open space with big green plants and a koi pond filled with orange-and-white fish. A small rock waterfall flowed into the pond and filled the area with the sound of falling water. I could also hear some soft flute music playing from speakers in the ceiling.

"Whoa," I whispered. "I didn't know there was a building this nice on the island."

"Crosshair is the biggest company here," Rain said. "They sell security systems all over the world. The owner is a crazy rich guy."

"Really? So why are we here? To ask for money?"

"No. You'll see," Juliet said sadly.

I followed my friends to an elevator and we all got on.

I don't like elevators—a heavy metal box dangling by a wire seems like a bad idea. It took everything I had to not complain. But I closed my eyes and pretended I was back in my bed in Ohio eating candy.

Juliet pressed the button for the fifth floor and we all rode up. When the elevator door opened, I got off as quickly as I could. In front of us there were two large potted plants and a big front desk. Behind the desk was a mean-looking woman. She had square glasses and an oval mouth that was taller than it was wide. Her shirt was buttoned up to the top button, and she had gray hair that swooped out on both sides.

"May I help you?" the woman asked.

"We're here to see Zeke Owens," Juliet told her.

"Zeke's here?" I asked Juliet in surprise.

Juliet elbowed me to shut me up.

"We'd like to see Zeke," Juliet repeated.

"First door to the left," the woman said. "Cubicle seventy-five."

"Zeke's here?" I asked again.

Juliet and Rain didn't answer my question, but they led the way, walking through the door on the left. Behind the door was an entire floor of gray cubicles. It looked like a boring maze that nobody would want to figure out. I followed my friends through the middle of the cubicles.

Juliet and Rain stopped near the seventy-fifth cube. On the side of the gray cubicle there was a small plastic plaque that read *First Mate: Zeke*.

"I don't get it," I said, completely confused.

Juliet motioned for me to enter the cubicle.

I stepped into the seventy-fifth cube, and there sitting in a desk chair and facing a computer was Zeke. I could see only the back of him. But I could tell he was wearing a nice shirt and a long pair of pants. He looked so . . . normal!

I felt nauseous.

Zeke was talking into a headset and typing on his computer.

"Yes," he said to the caller on the phone. "You can purchase the deluxe pack for only two hundred dollars. You'll never worry about security again, or my name isn't First Mate Zeke."

"Holy crab," I whispered with disgust and confusion.

Zeke spun around in his chair. His face went white as he saw me standing there. He sputtered and coughed as he quickly got off the phone.

"Perry," he croaked. "What are you doing here?"

"Sorry," Juliet said. "He made us bring him."

"You work here?" I asked my uncle.

Zeke nodded.

"And do you know there are a couple of lousy people in your house who were complaining about your towels?"

He nodded again.

"I don't understand."

"I'm staying with a friend," Zeke said sheepishly. "I'm renting my place out for a few extra bucks. You wouldn't believe how much people are paying for hotel rooms here."

Looking at Zeke, I squinted. I had never really thought about what my uncle did for money. He always seemed cooler than someone who needed to worry about paying for things.

"If you need money, I have a few dollars," I offered.

"Thanks, Perry, but I'm okay. I'm just saving up for something important."

"A submarine?" I asked, thinking it was just about the only thing worth becoming the first mate of a cubicle for.

Zeke shook his head. "No squid sub."

"Tentacle implants?"

Another shake.

"Ink implants?"

"No," Zeke said. "It's not important right now. I just can't believe you're here. Why didn't you tell me you were coming?"

"I wanted to surprise you."

"I'm surprised, but my house is rented out," Zeke said. "I think my friend has a couch you can sleep on."

"I'm staying with Rain." It was a lie, but I didn't want to ruin my dad's surprise.

Rain nodded. "That true."

"So, you're a first mate?" I asked Zeke.

"I started off as a deckhand. I was going to tell you and your dad about it, but I figured I would wait until I was promoted to quartermaster."

"I don't want to sound like a newt," I said, looking around and hoping I wasn't being too mean. "But this seems like the kind of place that squids go to die."

Even though I didn't want to sound like a newt, I did. It was just so strange seeing my uncle at a normal job. It felt like I had just found out that Admiral Uli worked at Old Navy—and not the cool old navy from *Ocean Blasterzoids* who fought in the War of Eighteen Kelp.

"Who cares about where squids die?" Juliet argued.

"Tell Zeke about what happened at the beach."

After first letting Juliet know that *I* cared about where squids die, I told Zeke everything that had gone down at the beach. I gave him the complete deets about the bunny bullies, the lifeguard stand, and the collapsing ground.

"Wow," a loud male voice interrupted. "That's quite a story."

We all turned around to see a large man blocking the whole entrance of Zeke's cubicle. He was shaped like a big squishy football, with small feet, a wide middle, and a tiny top of the head. At the tip of his noggin there was a thick tuft of brown and graying hair. His face blended into his neck, and his neck blended into his stomach. He was wearing a dark green suit that was the color of a ripe avocado. There was a name tag on his suit that read: Captain Fuzzy.

"Sorry to interrupt," Captain Fuzzy said. "But when I hear someone telling a story, I like to listen in."

"Fuzzy," Zeke said, sounding busted. "Sorry, my nephew and his friends just stopped by to say hello. I'll get back to work."

"First and foremost," he insisted, "call me Captain."

"Right," Zeke apologized. "Captain."

There was something about Captain Fuzzy that seemed familiar to me. I couldn't tell if I recognized him from some other time on the island, or if he just looked so much like a blob fish that I felt like I had seen him before at an aquarium filled with misshapen sea creatures.

"I'll excuse the interruption this time," Captain Fuzzy said. "Family is very important here at Crosshair. Besides, it's not every day that we get such famous visitors."

Juliet, Rain, and I all smiled nervously. The way this Fuzzy captain spoke reminded me of flavorless syrup. His voice had all the uncomfortable stickiness, but none of the delicious maple zing.

"I know all about you three and what you've done," Captain Fuzzy said, looking directly at me. "Saving this island again and again. There are a lot of people who are grateful for you. I myself was very surprised to hear that you had returned to the island once again, Perry."

"Where'd you hear I returned?" I asked.

Fuzzy coughed a little, sounding like Zeke had moments before.

"Maybe I used the wrong word," he said. "I meant to say I was surprised just now to see you here in your uncle's cubicle *and* back on the island."

I made a mental note not to ever take Captain Fuzzy at his word.

"Why did you come back?" he asked.

Glancing about, I saw the heads of other workers sticking up over their cubicle walls. They were all attempting to listen in on our conversation.

"I came back to see my friends during their bunny break," I informed the captain.

"How nice." His face jiggled as he tried to smile sincerely. "Children and their friends. Meanwhile in the real world, we adults have work to do. So why don't we let Zeke get back to his. I'd be happy to personally escort you to the exit."

"But we're not done talking to my uncle."

"Let me help you finish," Captain Fuzzy offered. "Good-bye, Zeke."

The captain waved at Zeke and then reached out to help guide me and my friends out of the cubicle.

"But the bunnies," I said to my uncle. "We need to talk about the bunnies."

"Really?" Captain Fuzzy asked, looking suddenly serious. "What about the bunnies?"

"There're so many," I said uncomfortably. "And well, they bullied us and . . ." I stopped talking because I didn't like the way the captain was looking at me. "Um . . . there're just so many, that's all."

"That's how the island got its name," Captain Fuzzy said. "I'm not one to nitpick, Zeke, but I'm not about to celebrate your nephew's lack of knowledge. Now, stop thinking about bunnies, Perry, and go do some sightseeing with your dad."

"Who said my dad was here?" I asked, shocked.

"Well . . . you said . . . what I meant is that I'm sure he is," Captain Fuzzy sputtered. "I mean, what kind of child comes to an island without his parents?"

"I have," I answered. "Twice."

"My brother would never travel out here," Zeke told Captain Fuzzy. "He has a hard time leaving his job."

My friends and I stared at the fuzz captain, wondering what he really knew about my dad.

"Zeke," Fuzzy said curtly. "You need to tell your family to leave now."

My uncle looked at me. His brown eyes clearly showed how sorry he was to have to be taking orders from a blob fish.

"You should go, Perry," he said. "I'll find you after work."

"There," Captain Fuzzy said. "You two have a plan. Now, let me show you the way out."

Captain Fuzzy escorted me and my friends down the elevator, past the koi pond, and back out into the bunny-infested world.

"Watch out for newts, Perry," he said as he pushed us out the door.

"What?" I asked in disbelief. "What do you know about newts?"

"Well, I know your uncle doesn't trust them."

Captain Fuzzy went back inside his building, leaving

the three of us to stand there looking as dumbfounded as the whale king when he lost his krill crown in Issue #10: "Born to Blubber."

"This isn't good," I said.

"I'll say," Rain agreed. "Usually I think you're just nuts, but this time I'm with you. That guy is suspicious. He knew w-a-a-a-a-y too much about you."

"And Zeke is no help," Juliet added.

"What about your dad?" Rain asked.

"What about him?" I asked back.

"I mean, could he help?"

"My dad?"

Rain nodded.

"Really?" I questioned.

"Hundreds of bunnies tried to attack us," Juliet reminded me. "Don't you think we should at least tell someone? Zeke's been helpful in the past. And since your dad is his brother, I'm sure he can help somehow."

"You don't understand," I said.

"What's to understand?" Rain asked. "Plus, it might be funny to see what kind of father a person like you came from."

Rain took off jogging in the general direction of the Bunny Hotel.

"I agree with him." Juliet ran off after Rain.

Standing there near the Crosshair Building, I looked

up at the weird sky and sighed. In a few minutes, my old life and my island life were going to collide when my friends met my dad. And I was not sure if I should run to the hotel or run away.

CHAPTER FIVE
NO HELP AT ALL

Typically, I don't like to go to my dad for help. He usually just gives me some unrelated answer that doesn't help at all. But we were on an island, and my uncle was being held captive by a fuzzy blob fish captain who knew about newts.

I caught up with my friends in the lobby, and together we found my dad in the Angora Room of the hotel. He was sitting down at a table and asking Summer what kind of plants grew best on islands. I stood next to him waiting impatiently for him to finish what he was saying.

"... I bet the sand actually helps the soil so that plants have room to breathe."

"I bet you're right," Summer said as if she deeply cared

about breathing soil.

Shaking his head, my father sighed. "Sadly, most people go their whole lives without knowing how crucial the right soil and mulch are to living plants."

"Not me," I interrupted them. "You told me on my sixth birthday."

My dad turned around. "That's because I thought you were finally old enough to hear the truth." He noticed Juliet and Rain. "Now, who are these people?"

I introduced both my friends, and my dad seemed overly happy about their names.

"Rain is very important," my dad told Rain. "There are very few things that grow without it. And Juliet was the name of the hurricane that destroyed my parents' first home."

"Sorry," Juliet said.

"Don't be sorry," my father insisted. "I've always thought it was the nicest name for a hurricane."

"Dad, can we talk to you?" I asked.

"I was under the impression that you were, kiddo."

My dad smiled at Summer to let her know that he was making a joke. Summer smiled back to let him know that she got it.

"Alone," I added.

Summer got the clue and excused herself to go do some of the work that she was supposed to be doing already. My two friends and I sat down next to my dad.

"We saw Zeke," I said urgently.

"Great," he cheered. "You didn't tell him I was here, did you?"

"No."

"Good," my father said. "Did you tell your friends about the Jell-O?"

My friends stared at me, looking like I had forgotten to tell them something incredibly important.

"I'm saving that for when I have time to tell the story right."

"Good move. Now, how's your uncle?"

"Not good," I insisted. "He has an office job!"

"Wet rotten wheat!" my father exclaimed. "I don't believe it."

"It's true."

"So, he's finally taking life seriously."

"I'm not sure about that, but he's definitely trapped in a job, so we need you to help us."

"Help you do what?" my dad asked.

"We have bunny problems," Juliet told him.

"I'm good with animals," he said. "When I was a kid I had a goldfish."

"These bunnies are different from goldfish, Dad." I looked around to make sure nobody else was listening and then whispered, "They attacked us."

"His name was Mark," my dad added.

"What?" I asked, frustrated.

"My goldfish." My father smiled at the memory of Mark. "You know, Perry, you might be ready for a goldfish of your own."

"I'm not," I said. "I'm also not talking about fish, I'm talking about attack bunnies! Hundreds of rabbits that tried to take us down."

"Yeah," Rain piped up. "It was ugly."

"Adorable but ugly," Juliet added.

My dad looked at all three of us as if we were smooshed bugs on the side of a porta-potty.

"What?" I said defensively.

"Good for you." He winked and smiled. "No wonder you three get along. I never could have made up that kind of thing."

"We're not making it up," I argued.

"Gotcha," my dad said with another wink. "Just make sure you imagine me up a little farm. I'd like to live in a place where I can get my hands dirty and grow things. Have you told your friends that they served wheat at the first Thanksgiving?"

Juliet and Rain stopped staring at my dad to turn their heads and stare at me. I couldn't tell if they were worried about how strange my dad was, or mad that I had never told them about Thanksgiving wheat.

"I never told them about it," I said. "This is about hundreds of bunnies that tried to do us in."

"That still doesn't make it right to ignore a historical fact like the first wheat. Did your uncle say when he would be done with work?"

"Later."

"Good, well, then if it's okay by you I'm going to go up to the room and rest. Maybe I'll stare out the window as I lie in the bed. The view of the volcano from my pillow is spectacular."

"It's a volcanto," Rain corrected him. "It's dead, so the locals call it Vol-Can't-O."

"Well, then I'll stare at Vol-Can't-O. Summer said the hotel is having a pool party later. Whoever finds the carrot in the pool gets an extra pillow for their room. That'll make the view even softer."

"So you're not going to help us?" I asked.

"I bet you can figure this out by yourself. Just think of how good you'll feel by solving your own problems." My father smiled at my friends. "It was so nice to meet the two of you. I particularly like your necklace," he said to Juliet.

"I like it too," Juliet replied.

Then, just like that, my dad left the Angora Room to go upstairs to lie in his bed and stare at a dead volcano.

"So, I think we should go back and try to talk to

Zeke," I suggested. "I knew my dad wouldn't be of much help, he's—"

"Um . . . sorry, Perry, but I can't go," Juliet interrupted. "I kinda have a job."

"A job? You're not old enough."

"I hand out samples at the mall," she told me. "My manager is mean, but she hired me because she doesn't have to pay me much. Also, it's Bunny Break and the mall's really busy, so I have to work for a couple of hours tonight."

"But . . ."

"I'm saving up to visit Florida next year," Juliet said excitedly. "I want to see what the real world looks like."

"Fine," I said, disappointed. "I guess it'll just be me and Rain."

"Actually," Rain said, "I'm out too. I need to get back. People will be returning their bikes soon."

"What about the rabbits and Zeke?"

Juliet and Rain looked out the front windows of the hotel. People and bunnies were moving up and down Rabbit Road without any problem.

"Things look okay for the moment," Juliet said. "I can hang out tomorrow."

"And I can do something tomorrow afternoon," Rain offered. "But you probably shouldn't go back to the Crosshair Building without us. Captain Fuzzy didn't seem to like you very much."

"Fine," I said, disgusted. "I'll go up to the room and stare out the window at the volcano with my dad."

"Volcanto," Rain said leaving.

"I know."

"Don't stare too hard," Juliet warned me.

Juliet gave me a hug before leaving. It was a small consolation prize. Nobody seemed to be taking things as seriously as I thought they should. It felt like I was living in *Ocean Blasterzoids* Issue #22, when the free-swimming giggle fish destroyed the town of Water Rot with their non-caring attitudes.

Summer walked into the room carrying bottles of water.

"Oh," she said sadly. "Where's your father?"

"He's looking at mountains."

"How serene," she said. "Are you coming to the pool party tonight? Finding the carrot in the pool is so much fun. I promised your dad a swim, but there will be plenty of time for you to swim with him too."

"No, thanks," I said. "If you do see my dad, tell him I went on an adventure."

My dad wouldn't worry if he thought I was doing something adventurous. The whole reason he had first let me come to Bunny Island was because he was tired of me always just staying in my room, playing on the computer and reading comics.

"Have fun," Summer said.

I didn't have the squid hearts to tell her that I wasn't planning on having any fun. I was planning to rescue my uncle.

CHAPTER SIX
ATTACKED ON A TRACK

I didn't have a plan. All I knew was that I was going to head back to the Crosshair Building to find a way to break Zeke out. I couldn't stand to see him trapped in a cubicle like the winter edition of *Ocean Blasterzoids* where cube fish were trapped in Ice Tray Cove.

The sky above me was filling up with clouds and getting darker as I jogged through the palm trees.

A cluster of bunnies hopped in front of me.

"Move!"

Two large gray rabbits hopped out of the trees and blocked the way. One of them turned its head to look at me and I saw its eyes glow red like the tip of a laser pointer. I stopped dead in my tracks.

"Soft soggy clam," I whispered. "What's your deal?"

The bunny didn't blink; he just kept his glowing eyes pointed directly at me.

I slowly stepped forward trying to shoo him away with my hands.

"Seriously, move!"

The bushes on both sides of the path started to rustle as rabbits by the dozen emerged from the jungle and closed in. I turned to look behind me and saw more of them coming in.

"I should warn you all," I yelled. "I'm recently self-trained in Cephalopodian Slap Dancing."

The bunnies drew closer and began to chatter and squeak violently.

"I don't want to hurt you," I tried to reason with them. "I've never really harmed a bunny before."

The ring of rabbits got tighter still.

"Okay," I admitted nervously. "I did have a rabbit's-foot key chain once. But someone gave it to me. And anyway, I threw it away because the fur made my eyes water."

The bunnies screamed.

All at once they leaped up and lunged forward. Their furry paws and heads pushed me down to the ground and covered me. They were so heavy that I couldn't push them away. A dozen rabbits pinned my right arm down.

I swung my body around to kick some off my legs and twist my arm. Flipping myself over, I tried to push up on my hands and knees, but there were too many bunnies and they were too heavy.

The weight of them flattened me.

I grabbed one bunny tightly by its leg and it screamed. I screamed right back at him, summoning my inner squid and flexing my skinny, tentacle-like legs and arms.

"Get ready to get squished!" It really didn't matter what I shouted because I was so buried by bunnies that all my words were muffled.

Just as I thought my life was going to slip away under a mountain of weighty rodents, the pile on top of me began to get lighter. For some reason, bunnies were jumping off and heading back into the jungle. In just a few seconds all the attacking rabbits had disappeared.

Coughing and spitting, I lay there alone, still holding the one bunny I had grabbed. A steady rain was falling from the sky and making my clothes and hair wet. It was clear now why the rabbits had fled.

The bunny in my hand wasn't moving. I let go of it so it could run off, but it didn't. I poked the lifeless creature and it still didn't flinch. As I poked it, I could feel that it wasn't a fluffy bunny. It felt more like a furry rock. Scooting on my knees, I pulled the rabbit closer and bent the bunny's leg. It was hard and clicked as I moved it.

"What the crab?"

I picked the bunny up and realized that it was heavier than twenty normal rabbits. Rolling it over, I saw a small seam on the belly. I pushed the fur aside and discovered a latch. When I moved the latch, the belly of the bunny popped open to show a small compartment full of wires and metal pieces.

"Fnaf," I whispered as I gazed at the robot bunny.

I inspected it as the rain continued to fall. It made no sense. My mind raced over the possible people who could have created it. Mayor Lapin had turned people into mutant bunnies, but he was in a jail in Florida. Lady Beatrice had created Big Bun, but she had been shut down. Or maybe . . . in Issue #37, Admiral Uli had had to fight off an army of metal marlins who had been built by Figgy. In the end, Uli had sunk all the marlins using sand bombs.

Standing up, I took the mystery robot and carefully hid it behind some bushes and two palm trees. I considered going back to the hotel, but I needed Zeke now more than ever. So, with wet hair and soggy clothes, I continued my quest.

CHAPTER SEVEN

WRONG FLOOR

By the time I got to the Crosshair Building I was soaked, a little nervous, and mad—soaked by the rain, nervous about getting past Captain Fuzzy, and mad at my friends for not coming with me. I would have quit my job to help them. Well, I think I would have quit my job to help them. I've never really had a job, but I like to think that I'd be really good at quitting one if I did. Heck, I'm not great at starting things, so ending them would probably be a breeze.

Entering the building, I heard the waterfall and saw the pond. The space above the pond was open all the way to the glass ceiling on the top floor, and the sound of rain hitting the glass was competing with the waterfall for biggest noise hog.

The Crosshair Building was cold and bland inside. It felt like a hotel that was decorated in shades of gray and grayer. It was all business, and the business seemed unpleasant and unimaginative. There was nobody around, and some awful flute music still played lightly.

I walked to the elevator and stood in front of it.

I've always really hated elevators. My dad always says that they are the safest form of travel after walking. I don't care: I hate walking too. I'm prone to tripping and falling. Besides, my dad sticks up for elevators because there are grain elevators used in the production of wheat.

"What would Uli do?" I whispered to myself.

For one thing, Uli would never take an elevator, seeing how there aren't any in the ocean. Their buildings just had things like buoyancy tubes, where you rise and descend depending upon the will of your gills.

I pressed the elevator button and the doors opened immediately. I don't know why I was so nervous. I wasn't doing anything wrong. Sure, Captain Fuzzy could catch me and then fire my uncle. But that might be a good thing. He didn't need to be working for the man. He was a squid, and squids are their own person, or cephalopod.

I stepped into the elevator and the doors closed. After I pressed a button, the elevator rose quickly. I closed my eyes and thought of things less claustrophobic and confining. When I opened my eyes, the elevator stopped and the doors split, and I stepped out as quickly as possible.

I could tell almost instantly that something was off. There was no big desk, no lady with square glasses, and no potted plants.

I had gotten off on the wrong floor. I heard the elevator doors close behind me.

"Clam it."

Turning around, I pressed the button hoping the doors would open right back up, but they didn't. Someone on some floor below me had summoned the elevator to them.

I pushed the button ten more times.

Standing there waiting, I felt like a fool. I looked around nervously at the small foyer with two couches and a couple of tables. Nobody was there, but I heard a voice coming from a hallway. I would have ignored the voice, but it sounded a lot like a talking blob fish.

"Captain Fuzzy," I whispered.

He was talking to someone about something important. His voice was animated and strong and slightly incoherent. I could hear words like *mess* and *Hutchman's* and *nom-nom*.

"It's a perfect plan," he said.

The elevator arrived and the doors opened. I should

have gotten back in, but I really wanted to hear more of what Fuzzy was saying.

He said the words *foolish*, *treasure*, and a few other things I couldn't understand. My tentacles were tingling, and I had to hear more.

Slowly I squid-toed down the hallway toward his voice.

"Make sure everything is ready," he said. "You must stuff every one of them."

With my back to the wall, I scooted down the hallway. I could see an open door with a plaque next to it. I inched closer until the words were clear.

CAPTAIN FUZZY NEWTON CEO

My three hearts sank into the tips of my tentacles. Captain Fuzzy Newton? Figgy Newton was Uli's nemesis, and now here was someone named Fuzzy Newton? Sure, I know the comics I read aren't 100 percent real. But there were times when the line between reality and *Ocean Blasterzoids* gets blurry. And now here was a blob fish named Fuzzy Newton.

I willed my hearts to start beating again and continued to inch along the wall toward the office. I had no ink blaster or steel-tipped tentacle. All I had was the Squid Tenacity body wash I was wearing. I thought of and repeated

Admiral Uli's motivating words to the Whale Calves of Coral who had accidentally eaten a shipload of baseballs.

"When in doubt," I whispered to myself, "blow it out."

I took a deep breath and exhaled before scooching even closer. Using my superior peeking abilities, I peeked around the door frame and looked in.

There sitting behind a desk was Fuzzy. He didn't look at all like Figgy, but it was possible that they were cousins or stepbrothers. I hadn't done a lot of research on Figgy's family line, but I figured that Figgy's evil family was filled with horrible freshwater creatures of all shapes and sizes. And Captain Fuzzy was definitely an evil creature of a certain shape and size.

There was a plate of food in front of Fuzzy, and he was eating with his right hand while talking on the phone with his left.

"This is going to work," he said into the phone. "Once the rabbits are engaged and set in motion, no one can stop them except me. Is everything ready at Port O'Hare?" Fuzzy took a few bites of the fried chicken he was eating and listened to what the other person was saying. After a large and loud swallow, he said, "Good, and warehouse fifty-six is ready. The Lost Hutchman's Booty is finally going to be mine. It's about . . ."

Someone grabbed me from behind and pulled me up onto my feet.

"Shrimp ship!" I swore.

Captain Fuzzy looked up from his food and glared at me angrily. A tall man in a green shirt and black pants was holding me up by my arms.

"Let me go!" I demanded, but the man held tight.

Fuzzy hung up the phone and stared at me with his fleshy face and eyes.

"He was listening," the man with the green shirt said. "I spotted him from the hall."

"Help him sit down, Steve," Fuzzy ordered.

Steve pushed me toward a chair in front of Fuzzy's desk. He shoved me down onto it and then stood behind me.

"You can go, Steve," Fuzzy said. "Now, Perry, what are you doing here?"

Steve walked out as I tried to think.

"Well?" Fuzzy asked.

"So . . . I left my glasses here by accident when I came to see my uncle earlier." It was a lie, but it was all I could think of. "I must have pushed the wrong floor on the elevator."

"That doesn't explain why you were crawling around by my office door."

I had to think fast. "I . . . I lost one of my contacts. I was searching for it on the floor."

"But you just said you wear glasses."

"Right, right, I had to wear my contacts to come find my glasses." My lies were hard for even me to believe. "So, I was searching—"

"What did you hear me saying?" he interrupted.

"Nothing," I insisted.

"I'm surprised to see you here," he said. "I thought you had been worked over by the rabbits."

"What?" I asked in shock. "How did you know about . . . Oh, I get it, you made those steel bunnies?"

"I don't know what you're talking about," he said, smiling. "But I think you need to remember that you are an outsider here. This island is not your home. You have no idea what's happening or how things really work. How would you feel if something happened to your uncle or father, or Juliet and Rain?"

Fuzzy stopped talking.

It felt like he was waiting for an answer to his question, so I said, "How would I feel if something good happened to them?"

The hair on top of Fuzzy's head seemed to sizzle.

I know that Captain Fuzzy didn't want to do anything good to my friends or family, but I had learned this tactic from Admiral Uli. In Issue #12, he kept acting like everything was positive as bad things were going down. Eventually the bad guys let him go because his positivity had confused them.

"Because," I continued, "if it's something good, then I'm fine with that."

"It's not good," he said.

"It's a surprise?"

"It's not a surprise, Perry," Fuzzy said, frustrated. "You have no idea what's happening."

"That's kind of what a surprise is."

Fuzzy growled. "Why were you listening? You know eavesdropping is a very rude habit."

"I wasn't listening, I was looking for my contact."

"Did you find it?"

I shook my head.

"Would you like me to help you look?"

"That's kind of you, but no."

"If you did lose a contact, then you should still have one in the other eye. How about you take it out and show me?"

I laughed like he had told a fun joke. "If I did that, I wouldn't be able to see."

"Take it out," Fuzzy insisted.

"Actually, they both fell out." I was an awful liar. Not that I lied a lot, but when I did it was awful.

"But you just said you still had one in to see."

All I could do was gulp.

"I don't think you know who I am," Fuzzy said sharply. "I own this building. There are over three hundred employees here, and they all do as I say. For example, if I were to ask them to help me deal with you, they would."

"Not Zeke."

"Maybe not Zeke," Fuzzy said sadly. "What a shame. I know he needs this job, and yet here you are making things messy."

"I'll go then," I told him while standing up slowly.

"Wait," Fuzzy said. "Maybe I should call the sheriff."

"That's okay. Sheriff Rolly and I don't really get along."

"That's right," Fuzzy gurgled. "You've caused trouble before. So how about you keep your nose in your own business and forget anything you might have heard today. It's the only way I can guarantee someone you love won't get hurt."

Fuzzy clapped and Steve came back into the room. Steve then escorted me down the elevator and out of the building to make sure I didn't attempt to see Zeke.

As we stepped outside, I looked at Steve. "It must be fun working here."

"Yeah, a blast."

I ran away and into the pouring rain. Then, as much as I didn't want to, I ran all the way back to the hotel without stopping.

CHAPTER EIGHT

DESPERATE TIMES

I don't want to disgust you, but when I got to the hotel I found a disturbing scene. The Angora Room was filled with old Bunny Mooners and tourists eating appetizers and shuffling around slowly. My father was there dancing with Summer. There was no music, but the two of them were swaying like there was. He was supposed to be lying on his bed and staring at the volcanto, but his plans had obviously changed.

Running up to my father, I grabbed the sleeve of his shirt and tugged.

"I need to talk to you, Dad."

"Perry," he said, smiling and dancing. "You were right about this island, it's enchanting. Did you know Summer has a brother that works for an insurance company in Boston?"

I wondered why my dad thought I would know that, or how that fact made Bunny Island enchanting.

"She also used to have a gluten allergy, but she got over it when she grew up."

"Congratulations, Summer," I said. "Dad, I need to talk to you."

"Let me finish this dance," he said happily.

"There's no music," I pointed out.

"And I probably should be working," Summer said. She stopped dancing and let go of my dad. "But I'll be done in an hour."

Summer walked off, and I pulled my father out of the Angora Room and into a hallway for some privacy.

"Zeke's in trouble," I whispered urgently.

"What?"

I told my dad a condensed version of everything that had transpired, from the steel bunnies to Fuzzy's phone call about warehouses and booty.

"Where does your octopus friend come in?"

"Admiral Uli's a squid, and I'm not talking about him. I'm talking about your brother Zeke being in trouble."

"Zeke's at work," my dad said, confused.

I slapped my mantle with my tentacle.

"I know you think I'm always making things up, but

this is for real," I insisted. "Just like the last two times I was here. Remember, things went down and my friends and I had to save the island."

"I remember you having some terrific adventures."

"They turned Zeke into a rabbit."

"I'm glad he got better."

"Dad, I really need your help."

"Listen, Perry," he said, putting his hand on my shoulder. "There is nobody I believe in more than you. Your whole life you've been different from me, but I've always admired it. You jump into things I can't even imagine. Now we are here on this island and you are talking about something that seems to be a problem only you could fix. A problem that . . . Wait, I forgot what the actual problem was."

"For starters, there are robot bunnies."

"There's robot everything," my dad said. "Did you know there's a coffee-processing plant in Michigan that's completely run by robots? It makes me sad that those robots will never be able to drink or benefit from what they help make."

"This is different, Dad. These robots are bunnies, and they attacked me."

"How?"

"Well . . . they piled up on top of me."

"Did you get scratched or bitten?"

"No, but I got some fur in my mouth."

"And my nostrils are dry," he said kindly. "Life's not perfect, my boy."

"What about the sinister phone call Fuzzy was making?" I argued.

"Perry, we're only here for a short while." My dad patted my head as if I were a dog he admired. "You should forget about these things and have a good time."

"You don't understand. I was—"

I was going to say more, but I was interrupted by the sound of someone shouting, "What are you doing here?"

I stopped what I was saying and rubbed my eyes in disbelief.

CHAPTER NINE
SOME SECRETS ARE EMBARRASSING

I wanted to scream with joy, but instead my scream came out as a slow, leaky squeal. There standing in the hallway ten feet away from us was my uncle Zeke. He looked wet and baffled by the sight of my dad.

"I don't believe it!"

My dad was upset that he hadn't been able to jump out from behind something and surprise his brother. But his disappointment quickly vanished, and the two of them hugged.

"I can't believe you're here."

"Well, I am," my father insisted. "I figured it was about time to see what Perry is always chirping about."

"Squids don't chirp," I corrected him.

"That's true." Zeke gave me a hug and then made a V with two fingers on both of his hands.

Without thinking, I did the same thing and then crossed my arms and wrists and wriggled my fingers to make the sign of the squid.

"I got off work as soon as I could," he told us.

He looked from me back to my dad. "I can't believe you're actually on the island, Zane."

"It's good for people to witness a wide variety of growing climates," my dad said. "It makes things—"

"This is great," I interrupted. "But we have a problem. There are robot rabbits on the island, and mysterious warehouses."

"Perry's been making up some fun stories," my dad explained.

"I'm not making things up," I said.

I told Zeke everything and then offered to show him the robot bunny I had hidden.

"Okay," Zeke agreed. "I'm always up for checking something out. You coming, Zane?"

"Um . . . I . . . well, the thing is . . . funny you should . . . ," my dad hemmed and hawed. "You see, I would love to go with you, but I sort of promised Summer that, well . . . I just . . . Summer, you see . . ."

"Got it," Zeke said kindly. "I know Summer. It makes sense that you would rather spend time with her than us.

Perry and I will do the sleuthing."

My father went off to find Summer while my uncle and I walked outside the hotel and stood under the large awning. We looked out into the rain and at the softly blowing palm trees.

"So, your dad likes Summer?"

"It's pretty gross."

"Yeah, we adults do some odd things."

"Like rent your house to weirdos?"

"It's just for a short while," Zeke explained. "It's a nice way to make money. I'm staying with one of my coworkers who has an extra bedroom."

"It's strange to hear you say things like 'coworkers.'"

"I know, but that's what comes with having a job."

"I never knew you liked money so much. I mean, don't get me wrong, I like it, too, but not enough to work for Fuzzy."

"Normally I've had enough work here to get by," he explained. "But I'm saving up for something big."

"And it's not a submarine?"

"No."

"A car that can drive on land and on water?"

"No," he said, shaking his head. "It doesn't matter."

"You're working for a blob fish named Captain Fuzzy Newton," I reminded him. "It must matter."

"He does look like a blob fish," Zeke said, smiling.

"Okay, it matters. I'm going to ask Flower to marry me."

"Whoa," I said in shock. "And you have to pay to ask?"

"Asking is free, but weddings aren't."

"So you're in love?"

"Something like that."

"I get it," I said. "Juliet kinda has a thing for me."

Zeke smiled. "Do me a favor and don't tell your dad about all this yet."

"My beak is sealed."

"Thanks," Zeke said. "Now, did you pack extra snacks for your trip here?"

"Of course," I replied. "I've got a whole suitcase full of them up in our room."

"Good. We're going to need a way to reward ourselves once we see this robot bunny."

It was good to be back with Zeke, even if love was sort of messing him up.

I counted to three in Cephalopodian. "Loo, ub, wel, go!"

We dashed out from under the roof, across Rabbit Road, and into the trees.

CHAPTER TEN

MESSED UP IN MORE THAN ONE WAY

The rain was keeping most of the bunnies off the paths. They were all trying to stay dry by hiding in the bushes and rabbit holes that the island was riddled with.

The path was also clear of tourists. Most people were inside businesses and homes waiting out the storm. If someone were to visit Bunny Island at the moment, all they would see would be a few bunnies and two soaking-wet people running madly through the rain.

"I never run in Ohio," I wheezed as loud as I could.

"I never run when you're not here," my uncle wheezed back.

When we finally arrived at the spot where I had

hidden the robot rabbit, my butt burned, my calves were screaming, and my lungs felt like sea sewage. I took a moment to hack and cough violently.

"Are you okay?" Zeke asked with concern.

"It's not good . . ." I drew in a deep breath. "It's not good for squids to spend so much time above water."

"Funny you should say that," he replied. "Seeing how you're soaking wet."

I stomped into the brush and leaves to find the steel rabbit I had hidden.

He wasn't there.

I looked around the base of other trees, thinking I might have had the wrong spot. But the rabbit wasn't anywhere.

"He's gone?"

"Are you sure he was here?"

"That sounds like a question my dad would ask," I said angrily. "Of course I'm sure. I was attacked, the rain chased them off, and I set the one I caught there."

I pointed to the exact place.

"Maybe he turned back on and hopped away."

"I switched him off."

"Maybe someone found him."

"Really? There's nobody out, and he was hidden. I think it's obvious what happened."

"What?"

I looked at my uncle with disgust. "Newts, of course. Are you okay?"

"I'm fine," he said. "I just have stuff on my mind."

"Not the right stuff," I told him. "The entire island could be in danger."

"Sorry, Perry, sometimes being a grown-up and being responsible take it out of you."

"That's why I'm never going to do either."

The rain began to fall harder, and the leaves above our heads plinked and plunked out notes that sounded like an ominous song.

"Do you hear that?" I whispered.

"The rain?"

I nodded.

"I do," my uncle said.

"Issue number twenty-three," I continued to whisper. "The newts used water drops on the surface of the ocean to trick Billy the Squid into going above water."

"That's right." Zeke smiled as if what I had just told him wasn't that important. "Now, let's get you back to the hotel."

"What?"

"I have some things I need to take care of," Zeke said. "I should be able to have dinner with you and your dad tomorrow night after I get off work."

"But, but, but what about Fuzzy, or the Lost

Hutchman's Booty, or the robot bunny?"

"The booty's a myth, and you and your friends can go searching for robots tomorrow. That might be a fun thing for you guys to do. Then you can go help the Bunny Break committee finish the rabbit for the bun-fire."

What was happening? Zeke was sounding less like himself than he did when he was a rabbit. He was under a spell, and it was worrying. He was saving money for a wedding, working for a man named Fuzzy, and suggesting that things like robot bunnies were not a problem.

"Fuzzy has a warehouse at the port."

Zeke looked at me and sighed.

"Look, Perry," he said. "I get it. The last two times you were here you did some amazing things. Now you're trying to find something that will keep things exciting."

"What?" I said, feeling sick.

"It's okay," he added. "You don't have to prove how brave you are. I already know you're amazing. It's okay to just have a nice time while you're here."

If I were a doctor, I would have insisted that Zeke was ill and needed to get help. He wasn't himself, and I didn't know what to do.

"Let me take you back to the hotel," he offered again.

"No, thanks," I said, disappointed. "I can get back by myself."

"Good," Zeke replied. "I have a couple of errands to

take care of, so I'll see you later."

I made two Vs with my fingers in preparation for the sign of the squid, but Zeke had already turned away and left.

I felt like I was going to blow chum.

A bunch of things were wrong, and a bunch of people didn't believe me.

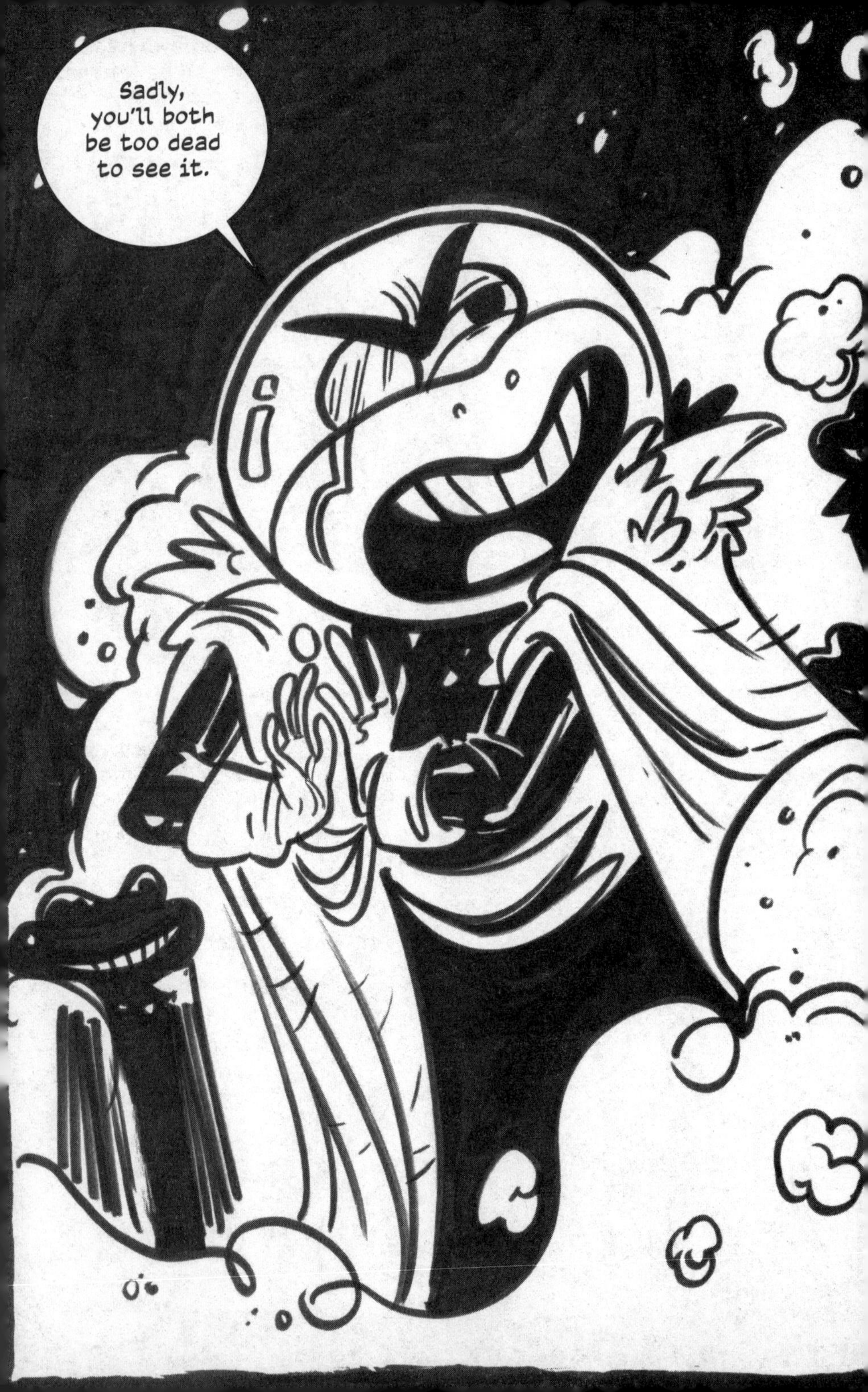
Sadly, you'll both be too dead to see it.

CHAPTER ELEVEN
TAKE THIS SOAP AND SHOVE IT

The Bunny Island Mall gave me the creeps. Not because it was the place where my friends and I had been turned into bunnies. Not because it had giant fake rabbit ears on the top of it. Not because I had spent time in the air ducts. No, the reason it gave me the creeps was because of the stores. Most of the people who lived on the island were old hippies, so it had places that sold things like high-fiber snack bars and cushions to put on your toilet seat. I remembered a store called Look Who's Old that sold ugly floral shirts and knee-length white shorts. I also remember a store called GrainStop that sold a bunch of those high-fiber snacks. It was the kind of store that only my dad could love.

Walking through the front doors of the mall, I froze. "What the wilted kelp?"

The mall had changed. For starters, it was super crowded because nobody wanted to be out in the rain. For finishers, it now had some normal shops. Not more than twenty feet away from me was an ice cream shop called Ice Ice Cream Baby. I could also see a hot dog cart called Doggin' It. The place felt much more alive than before. There was even a small electric train that drove around inside, taking old people and children for rides. The mall seemed like it was trying to step it up and move into the twentieth century—which was still a century behind, but very progressive by Bunny Island standards.

Moving through the sea of shoppers, I looked everywhere trying to find Juliet. I knew she handed out samples, but I didn't know anything else.

Just past the center of the mall, I spotted her. She was standing in front of a store called Soap It Up. She was wearing a pink apron over her shorts and T-shirt. She had a tray in her hands and was handing people small bits of . . . soap.

I stepped up to her, wearing an expression of concern.

"Perry!" she said with surprise. "What are you doing here?"

"You hand out soap samples?" I asked in disbelief. "Who wants a sample of soap?"

"Not too many people."

"That might work to our advantage," I said. "Because I need your help."

"I'm working," she whispered while checking to see if her manager was watching. "Ms. Purts will chew me out if she sees me talking to you."

"I found a robot rabbit."

"Could you at least pretend like you're asking me questions about soap?" she whispered.

"Right," I whispered back. Speaking loudly, I said, "Hello, I'm interested in soap. What do you have that might make me smell better?"

"That's good," she said softly. "We have some of the best soap in the world. All handmade, all-natural, these have cocoa in them." Juliet handed me a small ball of soap.

Lifting the soap to my nose, I tried to hide my mouth as I spoke.

"When are you done? Something horrible is happening. We need to get Rain to let us borrow some of his bikes."

Juliet smiled and spoke without opening her mouth. "I want to help, but I need this job. It's one of the few places that will pay me even though I'm not sixteen."

Grinning at her and trying to keep my lips from moving, I said, "So your boss is breaking child labor laws?"

"Excuse me," a thin man with a thin nose and sunken cheeks said. "Can I have a sample?"

The man took one of the chocolate-looking soap balls and put it into his mouth before Juliet could warn him.

"It's soap," she said. "Not a snack."

The man spit it out and walked into Soap It Up grumbling.

"People do that all the time," Juliet complained softly.

"Maybe they shouldn't flavor the soap with chocolate."

"I'm supposed to point out that it's not candy before they take it. You're throwing me off."

"Sorry," I said insincerely. "I apologize for wanting to save the island from robot bunnies."

"You know, if anyone else told me there were robot bunnies, I would think they are joking. But you're not that funny, plus the stuff we've seen makes me think you're serious."

"First off, I am funny," I insisted. "Remember that time I accidentally sneezed on that man's salad at Café Ruffage?"

"That was funny."

"Also, I'm not making this up. Just turn in your sample tray and . . ."

"Miss Jordan!"

My pleading was interrupted by Juliet's boss, Ms.

Purts. She had come out of Soap It Up and didn't look happy.

"People are eating the soap," Ms. Purts complained. "It's a simple job."

"Sorry," Juliet apologized.

"And who's this?"

"I'm a soap collector," I told her. "I was going to walk by your establishment, but I saw these interesting samples being handed out in such a nice way."

Ms. Purts looked at me like I was a stain she needed to clean up. "Really? Well, if you're a customer, either come into the shop and buy something or leave Juliet alone."

I was torn. I didn't want to go into the store, and I didn't want to leave Juliet. The safety of the island was at stake, and soap was bringing us all down.

"I guess I'll leave," I told Ms. Purts.

Juliet looked conflicted.

"Now go," Ms. Purts said curtly. "Oh, and Juliet, if I hear one more complaint, I'm going to have to let you go as well."

I looked at Juliet as Ms. Purts gave her the ultimatum. I'll be honest, part of me felt like this was all my fault. I summoned my tough inner squid in an effort to find the courage to set Ms. Purts straight, but Juliet beat me to it.

"Well, then how's this for a final complaint," Juliet said bravely. "Your soaps are oily, and they make my skin break out."

Ms. Purts gasped in horror.

"Here." Juliet handed her former boss the tray of samples. "It's Bunny Break and there are robots we need to take care of. Also, your shop smells like a hospital."

All Ms. Purts could do was stand there sputtering and twitching.

Juliet took off her apron and placed it on the tray.

"Let's go, Perry."

"Yes," I agreed. "I will take my soap business elsewhere."

I took Juliet's hand, and we moved quickly through the crowded mall.

"I feel amazing," Juliet said. "I hope I never see another bar of soap again."

There wasn't time to worry about Juliet's personal hygiene. We needed to get some bikes and get to warehouse fifty-six at Port O'Hare so we could put a stop to whatever Fuzzy was planning.

"Where's Rain's business?" I asked.

"At the back of the mall."

We walked against the crowd, past the Denture Depot and past the electric train, to the back entrance of the mall.

Outside there was a long overhang that was keeping the rain off a section of concrete. Wet air blew in under the overhang as water continued to fall in the parking lot and surrounding jungle. Rain was standing beneath the overhang next to six orange bikes.

"This is why I need to rent golf carts instead of bikes," Rain complained as he saw us coming out of the door. "Nobody wants to pedal and get wet. It's not like the water will kill you."

"I'm glad you said that," I told him. "Because we're all about to get wetter."

"What?" he asked. "Don't you still have work, Juliet?"

"I quit," she said defiantly. "I'll find a different job. Besides, who can work when the island is in trouble? According to Perry, Fuzzy has a secret warehouse."

I nodded. "Also, we're going to find the Lost Hutchman's Booty."

"You know that treasure's not real," Rain insisted.

"You'd be surprised by what I don't know."

"So, are you in?" Juliet asked. "I quit my job for this."

Rain looked out from under the overhang at the rain. "I don't think I'll be getting any more business today. Where are we going first?"

"Port O'Hare," I told them.

"That's on the other side of the island," Rain said needlessly. "Down the thoroughfare."

"Which is why we're going to need to borrow a few bikes."

"The rental charge is ten dollars an hour."

"I'll pay you back once we find the treasure."

"There is no treasure," he insisted.

"I'll send you money from Ohio."

Rain began to complain about how his bikes were his business and how he didn't want us to ding them up. He was acting like Juliet and I were a couple of untrusty newts.

We ignored him and hopped on the bikes.

Both rain and Rain pelted us, one with water, one with words, as we biked toward the Port O'Hare thoroughfare to find out what Captain Fuzzy was hiding in warehouse fifty-six.

CHAPTER TWELVE
CRUISING INTO TROUBLE

The Port O'Hare thoroughfare began near the police station. I had never traveled down it, but I knew it led to the other side of the island where the cruise ships docked. It was the only way for the ships' passengers to get to and from most of the restaurants and other things located on Rabbit Road. The thoroughfare was at least three golf carts wide and made from concrete. It had a bike lane on one side and a sidewalk on the other. It was almost completely flat and went straight through the two small mountain ranges on Bunny Island—the small Thump Back mountains, and the slightly bigger Volcanto mountains. Both mountain ranges were covered with lush jungles and small waterfalls that were easy to see from a distance.

I had never used the thoroughfare, because I had no interest in seeing where any cruise ships docked. In Issue #36 of *Ocean Blasterzoids*, the entire city of Whales nearly went mad when two evil cruise ships parked on the sea surface above them and played loud cruise music while continually dumping things into the ocean. Sure, it was a really preachy issue of *Ocean Blasterzoids*, and it didn't sell very well because the story was weak, but it had left a lasting impression on me. I had even signed the pledge at the end of the issue that made me promise I would never be the kind of person who throws things into the ocean.

"So, that's why I never throw things into the ocean," I shouted as we rode.

"Nobody asked," Rain shouted back, giving me grief the way best friends sometimes do.

The bikes made the journey way easier than walking or running, and the thoroughfare was mostly empty thanks to the rain. One golf cart passed us going in the direction of town, and two other golf carts passed us going toward Port O'Hare.

When we reached the port, we stopped under an awning on the front of a gift shop called the Bountiful Bunny. The rain was still coming down, and we were thoroughly soaked from our ride. In the distance I could see a cruise ship that was docked.

Next to the gift shop was a large golf-cart rental store

and a small café called Bunny's Burgers. Back behind the gift shop there were a bunch of big warehouses.

One of the biggest differences between here and the area by the mall was that here there were some actual roads. The roads led to various warehouses and up to the few surrounding buildings. There were no cars, but I could see some tractors and loaders parked near a couple of the warehouses. The machines were used to off-load things from boats that came into the port and then put those things into a warehouse for use on other parts of the island. The whole area felt industrial and not as interesting or beautiful as the other side.

"We need warehouse fifty-six," I reminded them.

"Down there," Juliet said, pointing past an abandoned brick building, and at the end of a short road there was a gray metal warehouse surrounded by a chain-link fence. The number fifty-six was painted on the side of it in black. Beneath the number was the word *Steel*. The warehouse looked old and weathered, with peeling paint and ample rust. It sat near the side of the Volcanto mountain range.

We rode our bikes to warehouse fifty-six and parked them behind three large stones and just outside the chain-link fence. The dumb rain was getting dumber and dumping water on us like we had done something to deserve it. Nobody was around, and the day was

101

beginning to shift into late afternoon.

We found the gate on the fence and were happy to see that it wasn't locked.

"Should we go in?" I asked.

Rain didn't have the patience to answer my question. He walked through the gate and over to the gray warehouse. Juliet and I followed.

There was a door on the front of the building, but when Rain tried to open it he discovered it was locked tight.

"Nobody's home," Juliet joked.

"What do you think's inside?" I asked, feeling let down by being locked out. "This place is huge."

The three of us walked all the way around the gray warehouse. There were a few other regular doors, and three large garage doors with ramps in the back. All the doors were locked. There were some windows, but they were too high for any of us to see into.

"I wish I had suction cups," I said sadly. "Admiral Uli would be able to get up to those windows and squeeze in through a hole no bigger than a quarter."

Rain stared at me.

"Fine," I said. "I bet if you got on my shoulders, you could see inside that window."

"How about you stand on mine?" Rain suggested. "I'm taller."

"Maybe you are at the moment," I argued. "My dad said I'll probably grow another five to six inches."

"That's great," Rain said. "But we don't have time to wait for that to happen. It's starting to get dark."

Rain stood near the warehouse below one of the windows, and Juliet helped me step into Rain's cupped hands and then stand on his shoulders. I reached up and grabbed the bottom of a window. Standing as tall as I could, I could see just above the windowsill.

"Holy hares!" I said loudly.

"What is it?" Rain asked as I wobbled on his shoulders.

"Rabbits," I exclaimed. "Thousands and thousands. There are rows and rows of them stacked from floor to ceiling."

Staring through the dirty glass, I could see that the entire warehouse was stuffed with bunnies of all colors. They were stacked tightly on top of each other, and all of them had their eyes shut.

"There're so many. I . . ."

"Hey, get down!" someone yelled at us from around the far corner of the warehouse. "You kids stay right there!"

It was a man wearing a green shirt and black pants and holding a rake. The surprise caused me to slip off Rain's shoulders and fall onto his head. We both tipped backward and plowed into Juliet. The three of us hit the wet concrete hard.

I could see starfishes dancing around my head.

"Get up!" Juliet said.

We all started running as the man screamed things.

"Stop! Stop! I'm not kidding."

None of us thought he was, so we ran as fast as we could to the front gate and out to where our bikes were. Jumping onto them, we pedaled much faster than we had pedaled when riding to Port O'Hare. We kept looking over our shoulders to see if anyone was following us, but no one was. There was nothing but wet skies.

"Who was that?" Rain yelled as we biked.

"I have no idea," I yelled back. "But judging by what I saw in the warehouse, we've got bigger problems than him."

The three of us pedaled as hard as we could, racing down the rainy thoroughfare and back toward Rabbit Road.

HAS ULI LOST HIS BRINE? ARE OUR SALTY HEROES BIRD FOOD? WILL FIGGY WIN? DON'T COUNT YOUR TADPOLES BEFORE THEY EVOLVE.

CHAPTER THIRTEEN
RAINED OUT

My dad was predictable and easy to find—he was in the Angora Room with Summer. They were sitting at a different table, and he was telling her all about the exciting world of being an insurance fact-checker. I didn't want to butt in, but we had an emergency on our hands and my father could no longer brush us off.

"Dad!" I interrupted.

"Perry," he said happily. "You're still wet." He looked at Juliet and Rain. "And you two are just as soaked."

"You need to come with us," I insisted. "Now."

"Where?"

"Outside. And you can't say no this time."

My dad looked at Summer. He then looked back at me.

"I'm serious," I added. "You have to come."

It was a surprise to all of us when my father stood up. "Okay, what is it?"

"Not here," I told him. "You're going to have to ride a bike. I'll ride on the handlebars."

Summer gasped at the thought.

"It's raining so hard," my dad said, looking out the large windows on the south end of the Angora Room.

"Pretend you're a plant and you're being watered," I suggested.

"I'll do it," my father said with conviction.

"If you have to go out, use a couple of the hotel golf carts," Summer said. "You'll get wet, but not as wet as on bikes."

Summer led us to the front desk, where she handed us the keys to two carts parked outside. We quickly found the golf carts and left the hotel, driving into the wet and stormy outdoors. Rain drove one cart with Juliet, and my dad drove the other with me. The carts were nicer than my uncle's old Squidmobile, but they lacked any fake tentacles or decorations. I wanted to drive, but my dad insisted I wasn't old enough. I didn't have the heart to tell him that I had driven the Squidmobile many times and in worse situations.

"Where are we going?" my dad asked loudly as we zipped through the rain.

"Just follow them," I answered while pointing to my friends up ahead. "I think we're heading to the Liquid Love Shack to get Zeke. He might be with Flower."

I wanted to tell my dad about Zeke saving up to marry Flower, but Zeke had sworn me to secrecy. And secrecy is one of the things in life worth swearing over.

When we got to the Liquid Love Shack, it was filled with people—some were drinking carrot juice smoothies, and some were just in there waiting out the storm.

I was thrilled to see that Zeke was there helping Flower.

"Perry," Flower said happily.

I tried to smile at her, but she was grinding a carrot and the image grossed me out. Seeing Flower reminded me that there are some adults in the world who are better than others. Her dark skin was speckled with bits of juice, and her long dark hair was tied up behind her head. She was thin and prettier than most of the other grown-ups I know. It was surprising that she was so kind, seeing how she was Rain's mother.

I introduced my father to her, and I told them all what had happened at warehouse fifty-six.

"Rain," Flower chastised her son. "You shouldn't be taking Perry and Juliet to the port."

"Perry took me," Rain said defensively.

"And now I'm going to take Zeke and my dad," I announced. "You're welcome to come along, Flower, but we need to go now."

"Maybe we should wait until tomorrow," Zeke suggested.

"Only if you don't care about the future of this island," I warned him.

Flower cared about the island's future, but she still decided to stay dry and stay at the Liquid Love Shack. My dad then drove one of the golf carts with me. Zeke drove the other one with Juliet and Rain.

The rain continued to dump.

"I'm glad we have this time alone," my dad said as we drove down the Port O'Hare thoroughfare. Fat raindrops whipped up against our faces and covered my arms and legs with squid pimples.

"We're always alone," I reminded him. "We live alone. Plus, we have a hotel room at the Bunny Hotel. We'll be alone there, too."

"This island is wonderful," he said, ignoring me as the moisture made his usually bushy mustache droop like a soggy starfish. "Intriguing hotel hostesses, and you making up all this excitement."

"I'm not making anything up."

"There you go."

"Dad," I complained. "Sometimes I feel like you don't listen to me."

"I have very good hearing," he said seriously. "My diet helps with everything from circulation to sound perception. People say I have the ears of a large monkey, and I'm assuming large monkeys have good hearing."

"Admiral Uli says, 'Assumptions make you dumbsome.'"

"The wisdom of a fish."

"Squid," I corrected.

The rain was getting harder and the sky was getting darker.

"I hate to be a wet blanket," my dad said. "But it's really coming down. Maybe we should turn around."

I was going to protest, but the sky opened up and rain poured down in buckets and barrels. The Port O'Hare thoroughfare was quickly becoming a river.

"Newts!" I swore.

"Where?" my father shouted above the sound of the rain.

"It's too dark to see any," I shouted back. "But they use the rain to travel in and drop down on unsuspecting enemies."

"Perry!" he yelled. "Now that you have actual friends and real island adventures in your veins, don't you think you can stop constantly pretending about squids?"

I looked at my dad and shrugged. "I don't know."

It was true: I really didn't know. I knew I was getting older, but I wasn't ready to abandon all the things that had helped me cope with growing up. Admiral Uli was more than just an old comic book character that a few people knew. *Ocean Blasterzoids* was a place to escape to and help me make sense of the world I actually did live in.

"I can't just give Uli up," I told my father.

"You're a loyal squid," he said kindly. "Also, I'm turning around. This road is a river. We'll have to come out tomorrow morning."

I was going to argue, but the rising water and the falling rain were about to wash us away.

My dad turned the cart around and Zeke followed our example.

I wasn't sure how to feel. I was worried about Captain Fuzzy, worried about thousands of robots, worried about Zeke, worried about lost booty, worried about the storm, and worried about my father always insisting that I was pretending.

I don't know which one of my worries worried me more.

"The Fuzzy guy who Zeke works for really is

concerning," I shouted as we drove back through the rain.

"In a perfect world, we'd have no concerns," my father yelled. "Of course, that would probably be boring."

My dad drove on as the sky continued to hose us down.

CHAPTER FOURTEEN
PAMPHLETS OF WONDER

With everything that was going on, I didn't think I'd be able to sleep. But once we got back to the hotel, I lay down on my bed to test the softness, and next thing I knew it was nine o'clock in the morning.

My dad's bed was empty, which meant he was probably down in the Angora Room eating whole-grain toast and keeping Summer from her job.

Getting up, I walked to the window and opened the curtains. It was no longer raining, but the sky still had some clouds. I was thinking of taking a shower and using the soap sample Juliet had given me when I heard a knock at the door.

I glanced into the mirror on the wall. My hair looked

like a sea urchin, and I was wearing an oversized *Ocean Blasterzoids* T-shirt that had stains on it from the previous night's snacks.

There was a second knock.

Quietly I moved closer and looked through the peephole on the door. The hallway was dark, making it hard to see much.

"Who is it?" I shouted.

"It's me, Sheriff Rolly."

I froze.

"Could you open up, Perry?" he asked.

"That's okay," I told him. "I'm fine."

I heard Sheriff Rolly sigh through the door. "I need to talk to you."

"My dad said to never let strangers into the room."

"We saw your dad downstairs," the sheriff informed me. "He's actually the one who told us to come up and talk to you."

"Thanks a lot, Dad," I mumbled to myself.

With zero enthusiasm or excitement, I opened the door. There standing in the hallway was the sheriff, and next to him was Captain Fuzzy. Seeing a blob fish so early in the day made me panic.

"No!" I said, trying to close the door.

I was too slow. Sheriff Rolly stuck his foot in and pushed it open.

"We just have a few questions," the sheriff insisted.

It was no use trying to hold the door closed—the sheriff was way stronger than me. So I let go of the door and stepped back into the room. Feeling like I might need something to protect myself, I picked up a pillow off my bed.

The sheriff and Captain Fuzzy stood near the mirror, giving me both a front view and a rear reflection of them.

"It's nice to see you're back on island," the sheriff said. "But Fuzzy here says you've been loitering around some of his buildings."

"He was crawling around and eavesdropping," Captain Fuzzy added.

"Crawling is a really good exercise," I tried to explain. "I'm trying to stay in shape."

Sheriff Rolly groaned and then changed the subject. "Were you anywhere near Port O'Hare yesterday?"

"I don't like cruise ships."

"That wasn't the question. Were you out there?"

"My dad thinks everything I do is out there."

Sheriff Rolly sighed. "I forgot how much fun you could be. Listen, Perry, how about you and your friends just try to have a non-lawbreaking time while you're here. Everyone already knows what you three have done in the past. No need to prove anything more."

"People keep saying that," I complained. "But I wasn't proving. I was crawling."

"Please," the sheriff begged, "just listen. Mr. Newton here isn't going to press any charges against you for sneaking around, but you need to stay out of trouble. It's Bunny Break and I have other things to worry about."

"And remember," Fuzzy said, "you are a visitor to *our* island. So keep your nose clean."

"I have allergies," I told him. "Sometimes my nose gets stuffed up."

The sheriff and the captain turned around and left the room.

I made sure the door was locked and then took a shower and changed into a pair of brown cargo shorts and an orange T-shirt with the picture of a giant squid on it. It wasn't Admiral Uli, but it was still pro-squid.

As I was getting ready to leave the room, I noticed the pile of pamphlets that my father had picked up yesterday. It sounds snobby, but I don't really care about the tourist attractions on Bunny Island. Ever since I first arrived, I've been fighting to prove I'm not some Bunny Mooner who only wants to see the rabbits and do touristy things.

The top pamphlet was advertising the hike to Bunny Falls. But sticking out from beneath it was one that said, *The Lost Hutchman's Booty*.

I pulled the advertisement out and studied it. It was an ad for the Lost Hutchman's Booty Museum and Cemetery. On the front there was a black-and-white picture of a man named Harold Hutchman. He looked like a typical hermit, with a long beard and scruffy clothes. I was familiar with hermits. Admiral Uli's stepbrother was a hermit crab who lived in the silt dunes near Briny Bay. Thanks to Fuzzy, I was also familiar with the Lost Hutchman's Booty.

The short version of what the pamphlet said is this: Harold Hutchman was one of the first people to ever set foot on Bunny Island. He spent all his time in the hills with his dog, Wart, searching for gold. According to the stories, he found a ton of gold, and by a ton I mean a dump load. He mined his secret mine until the day he died, hiding all the gold in a secret spot. After he died, Wart walked into town and passed away just outside the old police station. Wart had gold dust all over his paws and a solid-gold collar.

Ever since then people have tried to find Harold's hoard of gold. According to the pamphlet, the lost booty was worth an unimaginable amount of money. The pamphlet also invited tourists to visit the Lost Hutchman's Museum—a small, one-room building next to the cemetery where Harold Hutchman and Wart were buried.

I set the pamphlet back down on the table. If the treasure did exist, I wanted to find it before Fuzzy did. That way I could rub it in his greedy, blobby face.

I made my way down to the lobby. I thought my

dad would still be eating the free breakfast, but he was nowhere to be found. I was unhappy about his absence, seeing how he had promised he would go with me to check out warehouse fifty-six.

Summer was at the front desk, and as I approached her she looked up from what she was working on and saw me.

"There you are," she said happily. "Your father's outside waiting."

"Really?" I asked. "For me?"

Summer nodded. "I think he has a surprise."

"He's not good at surprises," I told her.

"Well, maybe this time will be different."

"Hey, Summer," I asked. "Before I get surprised, can I ask you a question?"

She nodded, so I asked.

"My dad said you grew up here, which means you must know a lot about the Lost Hutchman's Booty."

"Of course," she said excitedly. "When I was a kid I always thought I'd be the one to find it. I didn't, though."

"Right, but do you think it's real?"

"Who knows?" she said sadly. "Most people think it's just a myth, and some people have spent their whole lives looking for it. But that's not important now—your father is waiting."

I wanted to stay and talk more booty, but instead I left the hotel and headed out to find my surprise.

CHAPTER FIFTEEN

A SICKENING AND EMPTY FEELING

I was glad there was no rain. I was gladder that my dad was outside sitting in a golf cart waiting for me. I was gladdest that my uncle Zeke was there sitting in a second golf cart. And I was gladderest that Juliet and Rain were there too.

"I rounded everyone up," my dad said happily.

"I thought you had to work, Zeke," I said with surprise.

"In a couple of hours."

"How'd you find my friends, Dad?"

"Actually," he said, "they came for the free breakfast. I invited them last night."

"I'll go anywhere for free pancakes," Rain admitted.

"And I have nowhere to go thanks to you helping me quit my job," Juliet said.

"Now that we're all caught up," my dad cheered, "let's go see this warehouse."

I was surprised and happy that my dad not only remembered we were supposed to go back to Port O'Hare, but also seemed pumped to do so.

"I need to be back by noon to take Summer to lunch," he added as I got into the golf cart.

"Oh." It was now clear why he wanted to hurry. "What if this takes longer than a couple of hours?"

"I like to think positive."

The Port O'Hare thoroughfare felt completely different today. It wasn't raining, and there were numerous golf carts driving on it. Most of them were going in the opposite direction we were. Once again I rode with my dad while my friends went with Zeke. The air felt clean and cool from all the rain, and the sunlight lit up the lush green Volcanto and Thump Back mountain ranges perfectly. My dad kept talking about how he had never seen anything more beautiful or lovely or fresh or good at her job.

"Are you talking about Bunny Island—or Summer?"

"Both."

When we got to Port O'Hare, things were busy. People were streaming off the cruise ship and renting golf carts to drive around. The gift shop had tourists spilling out the door, and warehouse number fifty-six had two tractors outside it that were moving crates around.

We parked our golf carts near the three round rocks and then walked in through the gate. I felt like we were the crime squad or crime squids coming to bust a dirty corporation for inflicting dangerous robot bunnies on the world.

"This is the place?" Zeke asked.

"Yes," I said. "Prepare to be worried."

A man wearing a yellow hard hat and driving one of the tractors spotted us. He got down off his machine and walked up to us. From where we were, I could see that the front door was slightly ajar. I looked at Juliet and Rain. We needed only to push past Mr. Yellow Hat and we'd be in.

"Can I help you?" the man asked.

"I'm afraid it's too late for that," I said boldly. "The jig is up."

"What?"

Yellow Hat was playing dumb.

Zeke spoke up. "What my nephew and his friends were wondering is, what do you have inside?"

"Oh no," I insisted. "We're not wondering. We know."

The man with the yellow hat looked confused. It was obvious that Fuzzy had hired good actors to guard his place.

"I can't see why it's any of your business," Yellow Hat said. "Or why you'd care. But you're welcome to look inside."

"Oh, we will," I shouted.

Before anyone could say anything else, I dashed to the door and pulled it open as wide as I could so that my father and my uncle could see inside.

"Is this none of my business?" I yelled. "It's over . . ."

I stopped talking, because through the door it was clear that the warehouse was stuffed to the gills with . . . nothing.

"What the sea shelf?!"

The entire warehouse was empty! There wasn't a single robot bunny in sight. There wasn't a single real bunny in sight. There wasn't anything in sight. Just a couple of tables and a large metal cabinet against the back wall.

Everyone stepped in and marveled at the vast nothingness.

"I don't understand," I said dejectedly. "There were thousands of rabbits."

"In here?" the man asked. "This warehouse has been empty for months."

"That's not true," Juliet argued. "Perry saw them."

"Just Perry?" Zeke asked.

"Yes," I answered. "We were spotted before Juliet or Rain could look in."

"Are you sure this is the right warehouse?" my dad asked.

I nodded and mumbled, "Fifty-six."

"Listen," the man with the yellow hat said. "I'm not sure what you're doing, but you need to leave. There are no bunnies here, and this is private property."

"Someone moved them," I said, feeling my resolve return. "That's it. Someone must have moved them."

"Perry," Zeke said sadly, "if there were as many as you said, there is no way they could have been moved in the storm last night. You must have just seen some weird reflection or distortion when you looked through the window."

"What's in that cabinet?" I asked the man while pointing to the back wall.

"Not thousands of rabbits," he said. "Now out."

The drive back to Rabbit Road was depressing. I knew that what I had seen was real, but there was nothing I could do to prove it—the bunnies had mysteriously disappeared.

When we got back to the hotel, we returned the golf carts and Zeke and Rain left us to go to their places of employment. Luckily, Juliet was unemployed, so she didn't run off. My dad had his hotel lunch plans, but before he went in he challenged me to forget robot rabbits and try to have some fun.

"We're on an island," he said. "There are endless things to do."

"You've spent most of your time here in the hotel," I reminded him.

"And I think I'll spend some more."

My dad whistled as he shooed some bunnies away from the front door and went inside. I turned to look at Juliet. She was wearing her hair in short side ponytails, and she had on a blue T-shirt and green shorts. She was also wearing the kind of expression that made me think she didn't know what to think of me at the moment.

"So, did you really see all those rabbits?" she asked.

"Yes."

Juliet sighed. "Maybe I should start looking for another business that will hire a kid."

"You can do that when I'm gone," I said nicely. "I feel terrible about you quitting your job, but since you did, why don't you come with me to do a little sightseeing?"

"Does it pay?"

"No," I said. "In fact, it costs two dollars to get in. But I'll cover the cost."

Juliet stared at me in such a way that it caused me to keep talking.

"It'll be like one of those things that people do when they go somewhere, and someone pays, and they call it something, a name, a name that means that two people are spending time together."

"Like a date?" Juliet said, smiling.

"Your words, not mine."

"So it's not a date?" she asked.

"I don't mind if we call it that."

"And where are we going?"

"To a cemetery."

For some reason Juliet liked the idea.

CHAPTER SIXTEEN
THE LOST HUTCHMAN'S BOOTY

The museum was an old one-room house right next to the cemetery. It was back behind the airport and in the trees. It cost only one dollar and fifty cents to get in. Normally it was fifty cents more, but we got a discount because it was our first time.

After looking around the house for a few minutes, I couldn't imagine anyone ever coming back for a second time. We were the only ones there besides the short Japanese man who had sold us tickets.

The museum didn't offer much to look at. There were a few pictures of Harold Hutchman and a couple of his mining tools. Hanging in a glass box was a leather coat he once wore. And stuck to the wall I saw a few maps he had drawn of his mines.

"He wasn't a very good drawer," Juliet said as we stared at one of the maps.

"It doesn't make any sense. I mean, if they have his maps, shouldn't they know where the treasure is?"

The man running the museum was named Dillion. He was listening to our conversation and felt compelled to speak up.

"Most people think the maps are a trick," he informed us. "A deception. Harold drew them to throw people off the trail."

"This map is of the area out by the warehouse," Juliet said pointing. "Look, there're the three round rocks."

I could see Harold had drawn a mine opening near the edge of the Volcanto mountains and right where warehouse fifty-six now sat.

"I didn't see a mine entrance behind the warehouse," I told Juliet.

"Me neither. Maybe Harold drew it to mess with people," she said. "Or maybe it's hidden by trees now."

The drawing showed that part of the mine ran from the warehouse area back toward the Volcanto mountain range.

"Those hills are riddled with mines," Dillion butted in again. "People have tried to use these maps for years to find the treasure."

"Where do you think it is?" I asked.

"I don't think it's just sitting in some mine," Dillion said seriously. "Everything's been searched. He must have buried it deep in the mountain where nobody could ever find it."

After studying the map, I looked at a few small pictures that were framed and sitting on a table. There was a picture of the gold collar Harold's dog, Wart, had been found wearing. There was also a photo of an expedition team that had tried and failed to find the Lost Booty years ago. A third picture was of a man holding a bag and smiling. The small gold plaque on the bottom of the frame said *Fredrick Newton*. He didn't look like a blob fish, but I could tell by his face that he had to be related to Fuzzy.

"Who's that?" I said pointing.

"Oh," Dillion replied, "that's Fredrick Newton. He was obsessed with finding the Lost Booty. Forty years ago, he claimed to have found it, but after some investigation it turned out he was lying. The bag of gold he said was proof contained gold that was processed and brought from New York. He became a laughingstock. Nobody ever believed anything he had to say again."

"We know a Fuzzy Newton," I said.

"Captain Fuzzy is Fredrick's son." Dillion looked around the small room nervously. "He's almost as obsessed with the treasure as his dad was. Of course, his business has made him so wealthy, I'm not sure why he needs more booty."

"Maybe he just likes things that shine," I suggested.

Juliet and I went outside to the cemetery and looked at the grave of Harold and his dog, Wart. They had a big square tombstone with their names on it. Carved beneath their names were four words:

THEY DIED IN VAIN

"Don't you think it's weird that one of the mines ends right next to the warehouse?" I asked.

"Yes."

"I just don't know how all this stuff ties together," I complained. "What's Fuzzy's game? What's with the robot bunnies? And where did all those rabbits go?"

"And," Juliet said, "how come I have the feeling that you're not going to obey your dad and just have fun today?"

"Because you're perceptive," I replied, happy that she knew me so well. "Come on, I know what we need to do."

For some reason Juliet followed me. Sure, she was perceptive, but judging by her actions, I'm not sure she was wise.

CHAPTER SEVENTEEN
A SQUID, TWO KIDS, AND A CABINET

It took some convincing, but we were finally able to get Rain to let us use some of his bikes again. Well, it took convincing and twenty dollars. Rain tried to talk us out of what we were doing, but he knows how stubborn I am, so he gave up quickly.

"My mom will kill me if you guys get hurt."

"Then come with us," I offered. "Then you can claim you went along to try to help."

My rock-solid reasoning caused Rain to cave in. He put a sign on a bike stand informing any customers he would be back later and joined us on our ride out to Port O'Hare.

When we got to warehouse number fifty-six, we set our bikes by the three stones and then crept back into the trees behind the building. There was no sign of the man in the yellow hat, or of anyone in green shirts. We made our way to the front gate. It was unlocked, but when we tried the front door it wasn't. Rain and Juliet looked defeated and relieved.

"There could have been people inside," Juliet whispered.

"We can't give up," I whispered back. "Have either of you ever read issue number four of *Ocean Blasterzoids*?" I asked.

"Neither one of us has ever read any of those things," Rain answered.

"That's too bad. Because in that issue Admiral Uli uses a single spine from a tiger fish to pick a lock."

"Do you have a tiger fish spine?" Juliet asked.

"No, I have my dad's foot file."

I pulled out the thin metal file that my dad used to file down his bunions. I had picked it up from the hotel after we stopped there so I could get a drink from the hotel lobby and tell my dad that we'd check back with him in an hour.

"Eww," Juliet said as she looked at the foot file.

"Well, this eww is going to get us in," I told them. "When we were here this morning, I saw that the lock was super old. So . . ." I stopped talking and slipped the file in between the door and the doorframe. By angling the file toward me, I was able to push the latch bolt in and the door popped open.

Even I was surprised by how easy it was. And I might be wrong, but I think Juliet was impressed.

Pulling the door open, all three of us quickly slipped in and closed the door behind us.

"I honestly didn't think we'd get in," Juliet admitted.

"I was kind of hoping we wouldn't," Rain said.

The warehouse was still empty. It was like a giant void mocking me. Where once there had been thousands of robot bunnies, now there was nothing.

"Are you sure you saw all those rabbits?" Rain asked.

"No dumb questions, please."

"What's the point of us coming back?" Rain complained. "Were you hoping the bunnies would return?"

"I told you, no dumb questions."

"I think maybe you're losing your mind."

"No dumb statements either."

"Okay, so why are we here?" Juliet asked.

"Because sometimes cabinets can hold secrets."

"I thought you said, 'No dumb statements,'" Rain said, turning my own words against me.

Ignoring him, I walked across the empty warehouse and up to the large metal cabinet against the back wall. It was at least six feet high, five feet wide, and four feet deep. It was made of green-painted metal and looked to be just as old as the rest of the building.

"There's no way they could have hidden a warehouse full of rabbits in there," Juliet pointed out.

Rain laughed. "Are you thinking it's some sort of magical wardrobe?"

"So, you have read issue number four," I said. "Remember when Uli stepped into Davey Jones's wardrobe and went to Narwhaleia?"

"No," Rain insisted.

The cabinet was locked, but once again my dad's trusty foot file came in handy. I was able to twist it into the small key slot, and it unlocked. When I opened the doors, my friends were perfectly surprised.

"What is that?" Rain asked in awe.

After seeing the map in the museum, I thought there might be the entrance to a tunnel or some hatch where they had put the cabinet. I was partly right. With the doors open we could see the end of a conveyor belt that was as wide as the opening. It looked like it led down through a small brick corridor. There was a switch with back and forward arrows painted on it, and two big buttons on the side—one button was red, and one was green.

"It's a conveyor belt," Juliet whispered in amazement.

"Cool," Rain whispered for all of us.

It's probably best not to go through life just pressing strange buttons, but most of what I do in life involves pushing people's buttons. I figured it wouldn't hurt to hit a literal one. So I reached out as Juliet shouted—

"No, Perry!!!"

It was too late. I hit the green button, and the conveyor belt began to whir as lights hanging on the brick walls of the tunnel lit up.

"Wow," I said seriously.

"It's a good find," Rain agreed. "But I bet most of the warehouses around here have something like this. It's just a way to move things in and out of the building."

"Right," I said confidently. "Like robot bunnies."

Rain touched the end of the moving belt as it hummed and whirred. "Where do you think it ends?"

"I know a way we can find out," Juliet said.

"We can't just hop on a strange conveyor belt," Rain argued.

"Yes, we can," I argued back. "We have to. Fuzzy is up to something. If you had heard him in his office, you would have been creeped out. We've got to find out what's up before he uses those robots for evil. And it's not like anyone will listen to us without proof. Sheriff Rolly would lock us up for just being here. We can't get my dad or Zeke. Love has made them nuts. So let's ride this down to where it stops, see what's up, reverse it, and then ride it back."

"It does sound like something we would do," Juliet admitted.

"Great," Rain complained. "And when we get in trouble, I'll get the blame."

"You can blame it on us all being young and bored," I said. "Now, who's first?"

We glanced down into the brick-lined corridor and listened to the belt whir.

"What the herring," I said. "I guess it'll be me."

I jumped up onto the conveyor belt, and it pulled me down into the unknown.

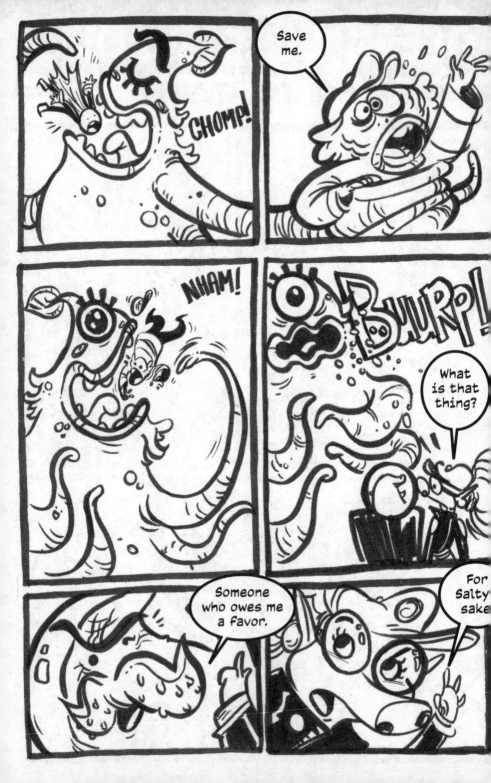

CHAPTER EIGHTEEN

CONVEYING FEAR

The belt was moving fast! I rode it down a slight angle to where it leveled out and then kept going. I sat on the wide black belt and crossed my tentacles while holding myself steady. The lights hanging on the walls of the long corridor flashed by me. I thought the conveyor belt would end after twenty feet, but it appeared to go on forever.

I heard Rain hollering. He was about ten feet behind me and lying with his belly against the belt.

"Are you okay?" I yelled.

"Nothing about this is okay," he yelled back.

Juliet was now down and not far behind Rain on the belt.

"Crawl forward," I hollered.

Rain and Juliet carefully crawled toward me on the moving conveyor belt until we were all close together. We weren't traveling at breakneck speed, but it was fast enough to make the three of us uncomfortable.

"Where is this going?" Juliet said. "I don't see an ending."

"Neither do I," I answered her.

The brick corridor was tight. There was very little space on each side of us, and only about four feet of room above our heads. We were all nervous, but the truth is that the ride began to drag on for so long that we all began to get bored.

"Are we there yet?" Rain complained.

"For the tenth time, I don't know."

"We can't be going to another warehouse." Juliet was upset. "We've moved so far we're probably under the—"

"End!" Rain screamed.

We had stopped paying attention to what was in front of us and failed to notice that the conveyor belt had come to an end. I flew off the belt and onto the tunnel floor. Rain fell on top of me, and Juliet crashed down on both of us.

The three of us moaned as we stood up slowly, testing to see if anything hurt. I had two scratches on my arms, Rain had one on his left leg, and Juliet was fine. Standing there, we could see a metal door. It looked industrial and had a large iron wheel on the front of it.

"Okay," Juliet said seriously as we all looked at the door. "Before we were thrown off the belt I was going to say that we're probably under Volcanto. But I don't know why there would be a door down here, or a conveyor belt, or us for that matter."

The belt was still running, and when I looked back I saw that, just like on the other end, there was a green and red button and a reverse switch.

"We could just change the direction and ride it back," I suggested.

"Okay," Rain agreed.

"Wait," Juliet said. "Let's at least see if the door is unlocked. It could be a way out."

Juliet stepped up to the metal door and turned the wheel. It spun slowly and then clicked. Rain and I helped her pull the door open. Behind the door was a massive cavern with a high stone ceiling. It was poorly lit by a string of naked lightbulbs hanging from a wire that stretched across the space and created as much shadow as light.

We walked through the door cautiously.

As our eyes focused and adjusted, we could see that all over the cavern walls there were thousands and thousands of holes. It appeared that we had stumbled upon the hub and origin of every bunny tunnel on the island.

"Unbelievable," Juliet said reverently.

Each hole looked to have a bunny butt sticking out of it.

"It's like Grand Central Station for rabbits," Juliet added.

On the other side of the cavern, there was another metal door identical to the one we had just come through.

The whole scene was amazing, but what wasn't amazing was the sight of Captain Fuzzy stepping out of the shadows not more than twenty feet away from us. He had sweat stains under his armpits, and even in the weak light I could see the perspiration dripping down his face. There was string around his neck with a thick cell phone–sized piece of red plastic hanging from it. I could see a single button on the strange red necklace.

"Fuzzy!" I swore.

Next to Captain Blob Fish, there were two men in green shirts and black pants. They each were holding long sticks.

Fuzzy's mushy eyes widened.

"Well, well, well," he said. "What have we here?"

The men in green pointed their sticks in our direction, and the tips sparked and crackled, filling the space with an uncomfortable light, sound, and odor. It smelled like the cavern had eaten something that didn't agree with it. We turned to run, but we hadn't seen a third man in a green shirt who had slipped up behind us. He too was waving a sparking stick.

"What are those?" I shouted.

"Let's just say they help us control things," Fuzzy said.

"Like robot rabbits?" Juliet yelled angrily.

"You three are unbelievable," Fuzzy growled as he stepped closer. "You have been a thorn in my side since the day Perry returned."

"Thank you?" I said humbly.

"What is this place, anyway?" Rain demanded. "Are those the robot bunnies in all these holes?"

"First things first," Fuzzy insisted.

The green man closest to us waved his stick and forced us to back up against the now-closed door we had come through. Together with the other green-shirted men, he tied us to the metal wheel. Rain, Juliet, and I were bound tightly, like three stalks of sea asparagus.

"You are so foolish," Fuzzy said. "Why couldn't you just have a normal Bunny Break? You know, play in the sand and ride bikes?"

"We did ride bikes," I told him. "That's how we got here."

"And how can we have a normal anything when you've tied us up?" Juliet argued. "Let us go!"

"That's not going to happen," Fuzzy insisted. "Do you know what's about to happen?"

"I'm going to wet my pants?" I guessed. "Not because I'm scared; I just really need to use the bathroom."

"Please untie us," Juliet pleaded.

"Yes," Rain said. "Please."

"A little accident is the least of your problems," Fuzzy said. "You see all these holes? Well, they are filled with X487s—or as you call them, robot bunnies. They are all quite lifeless at the moment, but this little remote will change that." Captain Fuzzy held the red piece of plastic hanging around his neck. "One push of this button, and all the thousands and thousands of rabbits my men have filled these holes with will be activated. Instantly they will begin to dig and tear through every rabbit hole on this island until they find the Lost Hutchman's Booty!"

Fuzzy shouted the last few words like a madman. He then took a few seconds to cough and wipe his wet, jiggly lips.

"The treasure's not even real," Rain said.

"Be quiet!" Fuzzy screeched. "Of course it's real. My father spent his life trying to find it."

"I know," I said. "He also lied about finding it."

"Enough. You could never understand how much the booty means," Fuzzy said. "There is nothing more important to me. My father discovered this cavern. It's a hub, a place where almost every bunny hole on the island runs through. My dad always wished that we could control the rabbits; certainly with all the holes they dig they must know where the treasure is. But we couldn't communicate with all those dumb bunnies. So I created a better version."

"Those aren't better bunnies," Juliet said angrily.

"That's true—they're *way* better than real bunnies," Captain Fuzzy insisted. "I've been testing some around town the last few days. That's how we've been able to keep an eye on things. I had thousands manufactured off island. They came in last week. Of course, you probably knew that because you were snooping around the warehouse."

"So, the place *was* loaded with rabbits just like Perry said," Rain yelled.

"See," I said defensively. "I don't make things up."

"Yes, you do," Juliet insisted.

"Quiet!" Fuzzy screamed. "You three will not ruin my triumphant day."

He stopped talking and looked at us. It felt like he wanted us to clap about his triumph, but not only were we unimpressed, our arms were also tied to our sides.

"This is really a dumb idea," I said. "It's probably the third dumbest idea I've ever heard."

I was tempted to list the first and second dumbest ideas I knew, but now didn't feel like the right time to tell them about my squid-scented clothing line or my squid-ink-based toothpaste.

"So what if the bunnies tear up holes?" I argued. "How are they going to find any gold?"

Fuzzy smiled a blobbaliciously evil grin.

"Perhaps you'd like an example."

The way Fuzzy was talking, I didn't think I did. But he clapped his hands, and one of his green-shirted buffoons walked over to the cavern wall and pulled a robot bunny out of one of the holes. He then carried the rabbit over to Captain Fuzzy, who took the bunny and flipped it over. He opened its belly and clicked a switch inside. Instantly, the bunny began to thrash and kick. Fuzzy set the thing down, and it shot like a hairy rocket directly toward us. Leaping from the ground, it bound up and onto Juliet. It tore at the necklace around her neck, biting the little gold moon with its teeth and yanking the whole thing off her.

Juliet barely had time to scream before the crazed rabbit leaped back to Fuzzy. He held the rabbit gently and turned off the switch. When it was lifeless again, Fuzzy took the necklace from its teeth.

"Hey, that's mine!" Juliet yelled angrily.

"You know the old saying," Fuzzy said with a sniff. "'Finders keepers, everyone besides me is a losing weeper.' These robots were made to find gold. Why do you think they chased you on the beach? Of course, those rabbits were set to the lowest setting. All these are now set to the highest. There won't be a bit of this island they don't tear through. All of them angry and wild until they find that gold."

"You're mad," Juliet yelled. "What about the real bunnies? The fake ones will destroy their homes and tear them apart."

Captain Fuzzy smiled a blobby smile. "Good riddance! They're annoying rodents anyway. And their pain is such a small price to pay for my immeasurable riches and immortal fame. I will have found the gold and avenged my daddy!"

My friends and I all *eww*ed.

"You still call him Daddy?" I asked. "I don't want to be rude, but you might want to work through that with the help of a professional."

"Quiet!" he yelled. "Or be loud. Who cares? Nobody can hear you. In fact, I'm tired of hearing you. So I think we'll go back into town. Maybe enjoy the bun-fire. And when the rabbit is burning and everyone is having a fine time, I will press the button and send the signal to start the rabbits."

"What about us?" Rain asked. "My mom's going to kill me if I get Perry and Juliet hurt."

"Well, that's your problem. I'm afraid I'm too busy to untie you."

"You can't leave us here," Rain shouted. "Those rabbits will tear this place apart!"

"That's true, they will. But I have to tell you, I can do whatever I want," Captain Fuzzy said. "I'm a grown-up, with money, means, influence, and a hunger for booty."

Captain Fuzzy and the three green-shirted men walked across the cavern toward the door on the far side.

"Good luck," Fuzzy said loudly. "And remember, sometimes sacrifice is necessary to make things better. Or should I say, to make things better for me? Farewell."

Fuzzy and his three men exited the other door and shut off the lights behind them.

Rain did some swearing.

I don't blame him. Things felt desperate. The three of us were stuck there in the pitch black, surrounded by thousands of bunny butts we could no longer see. We wiggled and struggled to get free, but the ropes were too tight.

"This isn't good," Juliet moaned.

"This is the opposite of good," Rain said.

"It's doog?" I asked.

"That's the reverse," Rain argued. "We're going to die and you're still saying things like that?"

"Sorry," I said honestly. "I really am, but if Fuzzy is going to set these things off during the bun-fire, we still have a few hours before this place is torn apart. Which gives me a lot of time to still say a lot of stupid things between then and now. Also, not to be super annoying, but I still need to use the bathroom."

"Can you hold it until we die?" Rain asked.

I clenched my bladder. It was the least I could do for my friends. In fact, it was the only thing I could do at the moment. We were in trouble, and for the ocean life of me I couldn't think of a single thing that would save us.

CHAPTER NINETEEN

WAITING TO BURST

It's not easy knowing that you're going to die soon, but it's even worse when you need to use the bathroom.

"I shouldn't have had those three sodas at the hotel," I admitted for the hundredth time.

"We agree," Juliet said.

For the last couple of hours, we had struggled and tried every way possible to get out of the ropes. But it was no use—Fuzzy's men had done a quality job of tying us up.

"I really wanted to see the bun-fire this year," Juliet lamented.

"I really wanted to live," Rain said.

"I really wish I could see anything," I complained. "I

never thought death would be so dark. I figured there would be schools of glow fish leading me to some shiny giant pearl that I had earned because of all my great deeds."

"I figured I'd die near someone who didn't believe things like that," Rain said sincerely.

"Maybe we'll be rescued," I offered.

"No one's going to find us," Juliet said dejectedly. "How could they?"

"No one knows where we are," Rain added.

"What about your dad?" Juliet asked.

"Really? He's probably lying on his bed and staring at the very volcanto his son is going to die under," I complained. "What about your parents?"

"My parents are always at work," Juliet answered. "They don't worry about me being home until much later than this."

"My mom won't worry about me either," Rain said. "She knows I'm always trying to rent my bikes. Now I'm not only trapped, but I'm not making any money. The sign at my rental stand says I'd be back two hours ago. It's like I'm lying to everyone who walks by."

Juliet sighed. "Maybe Sheriff Rolly will come."

None of us believed that.

"This is the sort of thing Zeke should save us from," I whined. "But no, he's too in love and busy working for the very person who's going to kill us and every real bunny here."

"This sucks," Rain said.

I sighed long and loud, like a blowfish filled with extra air. "I'm really sorry about all this, you guys."

"I know you are," Rain said, sounding more compassionate than usual. "We should have believed you about the robots in the first place."

"That's true."

"Besides," Rain said, "we seem to make as many bad decisions as you. I mean, who first suggested we ride that conveyor belt?"

"Juliet," I said.

"Perry agreed with me," she reminded us.

"I can't help it if I'm easily persuaded."

The darkness around us was suffocating. We could all feel a tension building, knowing that at any moment Fuzzy would activate the rabbits and bring destruction to everything.

Rain groaned. "So, Perry, what would your comic squid do in a situation like this?"

Things had to be bad for Rain to be asking about Admiral Uli.

"Well," I said, "Uli has a steel-tipped tentacle. He also has a beak he can chew through rope with. I'm sure he would have already gotten free by now and be home enjoying a cup of hot plankton."

"You're ridiculous," Juliet cried. "I'm going to miss that."

"I'm going to miss it too," Rain admitted. "I know I give you a hard time about all that crab stuff. But the truth is, you being you has made the island better."

"Except for this part," Juliet said.

"I had no life before you guys," I admitted. "Don't tell anyone, but you guys mean more than squids to me."

"Who are we going to tell?" Rain asked.

Rain was right. We were alone, and there was no way out of what was about to happen. I thought of all the things I loved and would miss. Thanks to my time on Bunny Island, it was a long list.

An inky darkness blacker than the air around me flooded my mind as the fear of what was about to happen crushed the life out of me. My arms hurt from the ropes, my back hurt from being crammed up against the metal door, and my bladder had had just about enough.

CHAPTER TWENTY
HAVING A VISION

In *Ocean Blasterzoids*, when someone dies they move on to a place called the Endless Tank Above. It's a tank as big as the sky and filled with all the things to make the after-ocean life wonderful—things like salt water, food, angelfish, and pearls.

Now things had turned inky for me and my friends. By all accounts, we were done for. But as I thought of the things I would miss, we all heard a loud clicking from the great beyond. The door we were tied to was being opened, and the ropes around us fell away.

Light flashed on while I fell to the ground.

I didn't see fish angels, but I did see Juliet and Rain, and my dad and Zeke.

"Is this the Endless Tank Above?" I whispered while rubbing my eyes.

"Nope," a voice said.

Turning my head, I saw Sheriff Rolly.

"Are you okay?" my dad asked forcefully.

"I think we're fine," Juliet answered for both Rain and me.

I wanted to point out that I still needed to use the bathroom, but it didn't feel like the right moment.

Sheriff Rolly and Zeke were looking up at the cavern and all the thousands of holes.

"What is this place?" the sheriff asked in awe.

"It's the master hub," I said loudly. "All those holes are stuffed with thousands of robot bunnies that are about to tear this island apart when Fuzzy sets them off."

Sheriff Rolly swore. "How do we stop him?"

"He's got a button around his neck," Rain told the sheriff. "If we get that, he can't turn them on."

"And where is he now?" my dad asked.

"He was going to the bun-fire," I shouted.

"Come on then," Zeke said.

We went to the conveyor belt, and my dad hit the reverse switch. He helped Juliet and Rain onto the belt and then pulled me over. I climbed on and instantly began to move quickly back in the direction we had come from.

Zeke, my dad, and the sheriff got on behind me.

"What happened?" I asked while looking back at my uncle. He was kneeling on the moving belt with my dad right in back of him.

"You said you'd check in," my dad answered. "And for some reason I began to worry."

"So you came looking for me?" I asked in disbelief.

"I found your uncle, he found the sheriff, and we followed the clues. Zeke thought that maybe you had gone back to the warehouse, even though you had been told not to. I also thought that, seeing how I'm your father and I know you struggle with staying away from adventure."

"I just figured you three would be doing something you shouldn't," Sheriff Rolly said.

"We came down the thoroughfare," my dad continued. "Zeke saw your bikes near those three stones, so we entered the warehouse and looked in the cabinet."

"It's hard not to jump on an unknown conveyor belt and see where it goes," Zeke pointed out.

"Tell me about it," Juliet said.

"It was a good ride," my dad admitted. "When we reached the end, we opened the door and there you were."

We told them everything that had happened and what Fuzzy was up to. Sheriff Rolly was shocked and upset. I was on my knees dancing to keep from using the bathroom.

The conveyor belt finally angled up, and we rose quickly to the cabinet, where we were then dumped out into the warehouse.

"When did he say he was going to turn those rabbits on?" the sheriff asked as we exited the building and got into the golf carts they had brought.

"When they light the bun-fire," Rain answered.

"Then we have no time to lose."

There was only one thing I needed to do before we took off. So, after a quick visit to some trees behind the warehouse, the six of us raced down the Port O'Hare thoroughfare, knowing there wasn't another second to spare.

CHAPTER TWENTY-ONE

URGENCY OF THE BUN-FIRE

When we reached Rabbit Road, there was barely any room for our golf carts to move. It was packed with people all walking to see the bun-fire. I was in the lead cart with my dad and Sheriff Rolly, and Zeke was driving Juliet and Rain behind us. We weren't really driving, though, because the crowd was too thick.

"What time is it now?" the sheriff asked.

My dad looked at his watch. "We have three minutes before they light the fire."

Sheriff Rolly stopped his cart completely while a crowd of people blocked the road.

"We won't make it on time," my dad said. "You need to run, Perry!"

It was a weird thing for my dad to say, but I had changed so much that for the first time in my life I was glad to have legs and not tentacles.

I jumped out of the cart and took off down the stone path, weaving and darting between people.

"What are you doing?" I heard Juliet scream from behind me. She had jumped off her cart to follow me.

"We've got to stop him!"

"Then run faster!" Rain yelled as he caught up.

It was hard to run too fast due to the mob of people. But I pumped my legs as hard as I could as I slipped around and through the crowd. I didn't want to be a squid at that moment. I didn't want to have three hearts and two ink sacks. I didn't want to live beneath the ocean and hang out with Admiral Uli. All I wanted was to stop one of the most unlikable people I knew from destroying thousands of real rabbits and their homes.

The tall wooden bunny rose up as we got closer. The crowd circled around it, chanting, laughing, and waiting for it to be lit. We couldn't run anymore; there was no space. People were packed in like sardines. Through the various bodies and heads, I saw Fuzzy sitting on a wide foldable chair surrounded by everyone. He was about a hundred people away from us and eating something! It appeared that he was enjoying the last few moments before the bun-fire was burned and he ushered in the reign of his robot rabbits.

A man who called himself Neil stepped up to a microphone near the large wooden bunny and wished everyone a happy Bunny Break. Neil was the president of the Bunny Island Chamber of Commerce, and it was his responsibility to inform everyone that it was time for the bun-fire. Neil was a skinny man. He had a gob of gray hair on his head and was wearing a T-shirt with a tie and shorts. A woman near him handed off a lit torch, and Neil raised it above his head.

The crowd clapped and cheered as Neil began the countdown.

"Ten!"

"No!" I yelled, but nobody could hear me.

We couldn't move due to the crushing amount of people. Seeing no other option, Rain and Juliet shoved me through a thick bunch of tourists.

"Stop Fuzzy!" Juliet yelled.

I popped through a dozen people and squeezed closer to the captain.

"Nine . . . ," Neil continued to count.

I pushed between two women and three men.

". . . eight, seven . . ."

A group of Bunny Mooners were blocking my way, so I spun around them.

". . . six, five . . ."

I dashed under the legs of three unsuspecting people.

". . . four, three . . ."

Standing up, I shoved my way even closer. As I pushed, I saw Fuzzy look up from his greasy plate of food. He saw me in the crowd, and his blobby eyes went wider. He held the red remote in his right hand and scowled.

". . . two, one!"

Neil threw the torch onto the wooden bunny and it . . . didn't light. Everyone was stunned, but the recent rain had made the bunny too wet. People began to boo as my heart lifted. This was just what we needed. Fuzzy wanted to set things off when the rabbit was burning, but the rabbit was not cooperating.

I looked at Captain Fuzzy, and he looked at me. Then with a menacing smile he shrugged and lifted the remote.

"Noooooo!" I screamed as I lunged in a last-ditch effort to stop Fuzzy. Unfortunately, I was too far away to lunge effectively. I flew forward, slamming down hard on the sand, ten feet short of him.

Captain Fuzzy looked down at me from his seat and smiled.

"Nice try, Perry, but you're too late."

He laughed aloud and pushed the button.

All around me people were shouting and complaining about the bun-fire not burning, but I knew that would soon be the least of their problems.

I stood up and saw that Fuzzy was smiling like he had just eaten the world's most valuable and important piece of cake. Juliet and Rain had finally gotten through the crowd and moved in to help me up.

"Did he press the button?" Juliet yelled.

I nodded violently.

"What do we do?" Rain asked.

"Yes," the captain hollered. "What do you do?" He stood up from his chair. "I have no idea how you escaped, but it's too late. At this moment thousands of bunnies are digging beneath the mountain finding my . . ."

Fuzzy stopped talking.

The crowd around us was still shouting with disappointment over the non-burning bun-fire. They were clueless as to the real problem. There were people booing and laughing and talking. None of that bothered me. What bothered me was the look on Fuzzy's face. He was chewing his bottom lip and looked worried.

The ground beneath my feet began to buzz.

"What is that?" Juliet asked.

Other people began to notice the buzzing ground.

"Earthquake!" someone yelled.

People began to scream and run, thinking the island was experiencing an earthquake. They were wrong, and as they panicked the ground began to buzz even harder. Then, like a thousand corks popping, bunnies started to shoot out of rabbit holes and leap through the air. A woman near me was knocked down as a rabbit clawed at her hands, trying to get her bracelets.

All over, robot bunnies were springing out of holes and tearing at the ground. They were hopping after anything or anyone that had gold on them. I saw a rabbit stick its paws into a man's mouth to get his gold fillings. Someone was screaming about their earrings and earlobes.

It was a bun-bardment.

The ground shook while bits of the beach collapsed due to wild robots burrowing below.

"You have to stop this!" I screamed at Fuzzy. "Turn them off!"

Instead of cooperating, he began to push and barrel his way through the frightened mob and away from us. Rabbits were appearing out of nowhere to bring people down. Real bunnies were hopping for their lives as the heavy fake ones blasted out of the ground and began to tear at people, plants, and soil in search of gold.

A black rabbit zipped past me and knocked over Rain. The scene was a mess! Only Fuzzy could stop it.

Juliet began to chase him, but she was waylaid by two bunnies that flew through the air and slammed into her legs. I stopped to help her.

"Don't help me!" she ordered. "Get to that button!"

I did as she said.

Using the kind of elite squid skills that only a true squid could, I slipped and squirted through the crowd, chasing down the blob fish. Fortunately for me, he couldn't run very fast or for very long. He knocked a few people over before quickly falling to his knees out of breath. I ran up to him and reached for the red remote that was still hanging around his neck.

"No!" he screamed, holding his right hand over the remote. "I want that treasure."

"Look around you!" I screamed back. "What good is treasure if you destroy everything?"

"Boohoo," he growled while still on his knees. "Not my problem."

"You're going to kill every rabbit and person on this island," I yelled.

"I don't care! The booty will be—"

Right on cue, a rabbit came flying through the air and hit Fuzzy squarely in the back of his big blobby head. The smile on his face was knocked clean off, and he went down face forward into the sand. He was out cold.

"Perry!" I heard my father yell above all the other noise. "Perry!"

My dad had finally caught up to me, but I didn't have any time to waste. I dropped onto my knees near Fuzzy and tried to roll him over.

on the controller.

My dad tried to help me, but we still couldn't roll him over. Fuzzy just lay there, facedown on the sand like a beached blob fish. Rain escaped a couple of attacking bunnies and found us as we were kneeling over Fuzzy.

"What are you doing?" he yelled.

"He's on the control," I told him. "We need to turn him over."

Another bunny hit Rain.

"He's too heavy," my dad said, still struggling. "We need . . ."

"I know what you need," Zeke said as he and the sheriff dropped down next to us. Together we all pushed on the unconscious Fuzzy, trying to flip him over.

"Push!" I screamed.

He was moving slightly, but it was taking every bit of strength we had. Also, it didn't help that there were still rabid robots chasing screaming people around and filling the air with sand and fake fur.

"If we don't turn these things off, this island is over!" Sheriff Rolly yelled. "Push!"

All five of us strained.

"Wait for me!" Juliet shouted.

She dropped down and leveraged her arms to help

push up as we pushed over. The six of us gave it everything we had. Fuzzy turned just enough so that I could
reach under him and grab the remote.

I yanked it off his neck with one hand as we let him
drop back onto his stomach.

"Press the button!" my dad yelled.

My life was usually better when I did what my dad
suggested, so I pressed the button and . . . nothing happened.

"Press it again!" Zeke shouted.

I pressed it ten more times, but it still didn't do anything.

"Maybe it takes a fingerprint!" Juliet said. "My mother's cell phones can do that."

Sheriff Rolly grabbed Fuzzy's right arm as he lay on
the sand. He then shoved Fuzzy's pointer finger onto the
button as I held the remote.

Nothing happened!

"I think his finger's too greasy to read the fingerprint!" I told them. "Wipe it off."

"Gross!" Rain complained as a rabbit ran up his back
and jumped onto a screaming lady who was trying to
protect her gold earrings.

Zeke grabbed Fuzzy's hand from Sheriff Rolly and
wiped his finger on his own T-shirt. The sheriff then
tried again by smashing the finger onto the button.

This time it worked!

All at once, every robot rabbit shut down. Bunnies in midleap fell to the ground. They all stopped what they were doing and instantly became furry, lifeless hunks of metal and hair.

Juliet began to jump with joy. She hugged me so long that I did a little joy jumping (and some crying as well). Sheriff Rolly instantly got up and went about trying to calm the crowd down as everyone on the island tried to figure out what the heck had just happened. The bunfire statue had been trampled by all the action and was now just a large pile of wood.

"Perry," I heard my father say.

I turned around, and he patted me on the shoulder in a way that made me feel as if he approved of everything that I had ever done. Zeke was next to him smiling proudly.

"What do you think of Bunny Island?" I asked my dad.

"It's spectacular," he said with excitement. "Of course, what I'm most impressed with is you."

"I told you," my uncle Zeke said to his brother. "This island needs Perry."

"Well, I'd be dead if you hadn't come looking for me," I reminded them.

"Just know that I always will," my dad said.

"Actually," Zeke said as he looked around at the confused, loud, and crazy scene, "you both picked the perfect time to visit. Bunny Break is always fun."

I looked around at the disoriented tourists and Bunny Mooners and the hundreds of robot bunnies lying on the ground.

As usual, Bunny Island had not disappointed.

CHAPTER TWENTY-TWO

WHEN ALL THE SEA SALT SETTLES

It's been three months since we were almost bunnied to death. Sheriff Rolly arrested Fuzzy. He was charged with a list of very serious things, not the least of which was trying to put an end to me and my friends. He would be locked up for a long while. His business went bankrupt, and his things were repossessed to pay for the damage his rabbits did.

I'm not sad about any of that.

Of course, my life is pretty different than it used to be. The biggest difference is that I no longer live in Ohio. Nope, my dad fell in love with the island and with Summer. So he moved the two of us out here a month ago.

We bought a small lima bean farm near Bunny Cove. He and Zeke are going to make a living by being bean farmers.

Yep, Bunny Island is my home now. I have to say that I'm happy about that. I don't miss much about Ohio. Sure, there was a great comic book shop back in my town. And yes, they have way more junk food, but the trade-off is worth it. I have my friends and all the adventure I could ever want.

To this day, nobody's found the Lost Hutchman's Booty. Rain continues to insist that it never existed, but that hasn't stopped Juliet and me from spending time hiking around the island and trying to find it.

Of course, the new thing for people to search for around here is lifeless robot bunnies. There are still thousands hidden all over the island. They're highly collectible souvenirs and have provided Bunny Island with another unusual layer.

I don't think I've ever come to Bunny Island looking for trouble. The first time I came I was on a rescue mission, but my intention was just to find my uncle. I never wanted to do things like run and fight to stay alive. My dad had hoped I would find adventure, but my dad was just a single dad who wanted his son to get out of the house and have a childhood he would remember. Well, I'll never forget the things that have happened here. At the very least, it's taught me that there is just as much to get excited about above water as there is down below.

I don't have to run everywhere these days. My dad bought Summer a golf cart, and she lets me drive it whenever I want. Which is why I was now driving down Rabbit Road and stopping in front of the Liquid Love Shack.

Juliet was standing out front with Rain. They were both wearing long pants and nice shirts. I had never seen them look so dressed up. I smiled as they climbed onto the cart. Rain sat in the backseat next to a box wrapped in red paper.

"You look just as funny," Rain said to me.

He was right. I also had on long pants and a nice shirt, part of a whole outfit my dad had bought me.

"So, are you ready for this?" Juliet asked. "I mean, Summer's going to be your stepmom."

"What about me?" Rain asked as we drove down Rabbit Road toward the beach. "With Zeke marrying my mom, it's almost like Perry and I are related."

"It's almost like you won something," I said.

Yes, both my dad and my uncle were getting married today—a double wedding taking place down on the shore.

"I'll be honest," Rain admitted. "I never saw this happening."

ell, _ _ i sa _ m _ _ ot _ _t _ _ p_
but I personally think things are just as they should be."

I looked up at the sky as I drove. It was filled with white fluffy clouds. I saw some that looked like bunnies, one that looked like a carrot, and one that looked like a squid. I had changed a lot in the last while. Maybe Admiral Uli and all his world exist only in comics, but for me they will always be the very real thing that inspired me to make the trip to Bunny Island in the first place.

And just to be safe, I will always be on the lookout for newts.

Juliet saw the squid-shaped cloud and smiled at me. She was right: things were just as they should be.

"So, what's this?" Rain asked, picking up the wrapped red box next to him.

"That's my dad's wedding present to Zeke," I answered.

Juliet turned to look at the box. "What is it?"

"Shoes."

Rain laughed. "Your dad is giving Zeke shoes for his wedding gift? That's not normal."

"They're filled with Jell-O," I added.

"That sounds about right," Juliet said happily.

I pressed on the gas, and we raced to the beach going seven miles an hour. Above us the clouds broke apart and enc poss ies.

Luckily, I didn't need to be an admiral or a squid to realize that.

ACKNOWLEDGMENTS

People are great. However, some people are greater. One of those greater people is my editor, David Linker. Thanks for getting your hands dirty and molding these books into what they are—you are magical and kind. Thanks as well to my agent Laurie for making this possible. Thanks to Tiffany Liao and Abby Ranger—you were there at the start and hold a special place in my heart (rhyme intended). Thanks to HarperCollins and the amazing work they do. Thanks to Eduardo Vieira. Your art and talent have brought Uli to life in a spectacular way. And thanks to Krista. Sure, I've thanked you a million times, but it still seems insufficient.

MORE BOOKS IN THE MUTANT BUNNY ISLAND SERIES!

HARPER
An Imprint of HarperCollinsPublishers
WWW.HARPERCOLLINSCHILDRENS.COM

MORE BOOKS IN THE
HAMSTERSAURUS REX SERIES!

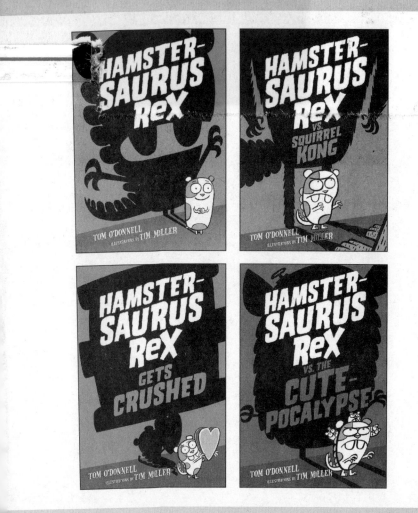

31901065377469